THE LANCES OF LYNWOOD

by
CHARLOTTE M. YONGE

2

PREFACE

For an explanation of the allusions in the present Tale, scarcely any Notes are necessary, save a reference to the bewitching Chronicle of Froissart; and we cannot but hope that our sketch may serve as an inducement to some young readers to make acquaintance with the delectable old Canon for themselves, undeterred by the size of his tomes.

The story of Orthon is almost verbally copied from him, and bears a curious resemblance to various German legends—such as that of "Heinzelman," to be found in Keightley's "Fairy Mythology," and to "Teague of the Lea," as related in Croker's "Irish Fairy Legends."

The old French "Vie de Bertrand du Guesclin" has likewise been drawn upon for materials, and would have supplied much more of great interest, such as Enrique of Trastamare's arrival in the disguise of a palmer, to consult with him during his captivity at Bordeaux, and many most curious anecdotes of his early childhood and youth.

To Breton tradition, his excellent wife Epiphanie Raguenel owes her title of Tiphaine la fee, meaning that she was endowed with magic power, which enabled her to predict what would be lucky or unlucky days for her husband. His disregard of them was thought to have twice cost him the loss of a battle.

We must apologize for having made Henry of Lancaster a year or two older than is warranted by the date of his birth.

CHAPTER I

Seldom had the interior of this island presented a more peaceful and prosperous aspect than in the reign of Edward III., when the more turbulent spirits among his subjects had found occupation in his foreign wars, and his wise government had established at home a degree of plenty, tranquility, and security, such as had probably never before been experienced in England.

Castle and cottage, church and convent, alike showed the prosperity and safety of the inhabitants, at once by the profuseness of embellishment in those newly erected, and by the neglect of the jealous precautions required in former days of confusion and misrule. Thus it was with the village of Lynwood, where, among the cottages and farm-houses occupying a fertile valley in Somersetshire, arose the ancient Keep, built of gray stone, and strongly fortified; but the defences were kept up rather as appendages of the owner's rank, than as requisite for his protection; though the moat was clear of weeds, and full of water, the drawbridge was so well covered with hard-trodden earth, overgrown at the edges with grass, that, in spite of the massive chains connecting it with the gateway, it seemed permanently fixed on the ground. The spikes of the portcullis frowned above in threatening array, but a wreath of ivy was twining up the groove by which it had

3

once descended, and the archway, which by day stood hospitably open, was at night only guarded by two large oaken doors, yielding to a slight push. Beneath the southern wall of the castle court were various flower-beds, the pride and delight of the old seneschal, Ralph Penrose, in his own estimation the most important personage of Lynwood Keep, manager of the servants, adviser of the Lady, and instructor of the young gentleman in the exercises of chivalry.

One fine evening, old Ralph stood before the door, his bald forehead and thin iron-gray locks unbonneted, and his dark ruddy-brown face (marked at Halidon Hill with a deep scar) raised with an air of deference, and yet of self-satisfaction, towards the Lady who stood on the steps of the porch. She was small and fragile in figure; her face, though very lovely, was pale and thin, and her smile had in it something pensive and almost melancholy, as she listened to his narration of his dealings with a refractory tenant, and at the same time watched a noble-looking child of seven or eight years old, who, mounted on an old war-horse, was led round the court by a youth, his elder by some ten or eleven years.

"See mother!" cried the child, "I am holding the reins myself. Uncle Eustace lays not a finger on them!"

"As I was saying, madam," continued Ralph, disregarding the interruption, "I told him that I should not have thought of one exempted from feudal service in the camp, by our noble Knight, being deficient in his dues in his absence. I told him we should see how he liked to be sent packing to Bordeaux with a sheaf of arrows on his back, instead of the sheaf of wheat which ought to be in our granary by this time. But you are too gentle with them, my Lady, and they grow insolent in Sir Reginald's long absence."

"All goes ill in his absence," said the Lady. "It is a weary while since the wounded archer brought tidings of his speedy return."

"Therefore," said the youth, turning round, "it must be the nearer at hand. Come sweet sister Eleanor, cheer up, for he cannot but come soon."

"So many *soons* have passed away, that my heart is well-nigh too sick for hope," said Eleanor. "And when he comes it will be but a bright dream to last for a moment. He cannot long be spared from the Prince's side."

"You must go with him, then, sister, and see how I begin my days of chivalry—that is, if he will but believe me fit to bear shield and lance."

"Ah! Master Eustace, if you were but such as I have seen others of your race," said Ralph, shaking his head. "There was Sir Henry—at your age he had made the Scottish thieves look about them, I promise you. And to go no further back than Sir Reginald himself—he stood by the Prince's side at Crecy ere he was yet fifteen!"

"It is not my fault that I have not done as much, Ralph," said Eustace. "It is not for want of the will, as you know full well."

"No. Thanks to me, I trust you have the will and the teaching, at least, to make a good Knight," said Ralph. "And yet, while I think of the goodly height and broad shoulders of those that have gone before you—"

"But hark! hark!" cried Eustace, cutting short a comparison which did not seem likely to be complimentary. "Dost not hear, Ralph? A horn!"

4

"The Lynwood note! My husband's note! O thanks, thanks to the Saints!" cried the Lady, clasping her hands, whilst Eustace, vaulting into the saddle behind his little nephew, rode across the drawbridge as fast as the stiffened joints of old Blanc Etoile could be prevailed on to move. Gaining the summit of a rising ground, both at once shouted, "Our own pennon! It is himself!" as they beheld the dark blue crosslet on an argent field floating above a troop of horsemen, whose armour glanced in the setting sun.

"There are the Lances of Lynwood, Arthur," said Eustace, leaping to the ground. "Keep your seat, and meet your father like a brave Knight's son."

He then settled the reins in the child's hand, and walked beside him to meet the new-comers. They were about twenty in number, armed alike with corselets marked with the blue cross, steel headpieces, and long lances. In front rode two of higher rank. The first was a man of noble mien and lofty stature, his short dark curled hair and beard, and handsome though sunburnt countenance, displayed beneath his small blue velvet cap, his helmet being carried behind him by a man-at-arms, and his attire consisting of a close-fitting dress of chamois leather, a white mantle embroidered with the blue cross thrown over one shoulder, and his sword hanging by his side. His companion, who carried at his saddle-bow a shield blazoned with heraldic devices in scarlet and gold, was of still greater height, and very slight; his large keen eyes, hair and moustache, black as jet; and his complexion dark brown, with a well-formed aquiline nose, and a perfect and very white set of teeth.

The instant the first-mentioned horseman perceived Eustace and Arthur, he sprang to the ground and hurried to meet them with rapid affectionate greetings and inquiries. In another moment Dame Eleanor appeared on the drawbridge, and, weeping with joy, was clasped in her husband's arms. Behind her stood the venerable chaplain, Father Cyril, and a step or two further off, Ralph Penrose, both of whom in turn received the kindly greetings of Sir Reginald Lynwood, as, with his wife hanging on his arm and his boy holding his hand, he passed under the gateway of his ancestral castle. Turning the next moment, he addressed his tall companion: "Friend Gaston, I bid you welcome! Dame Eleanor, and you, brother Eustace, I present to you my trusty Esquire, Master Gaston d'Aubricour."

Due courtesies passed between the Lady and the Squire, who, after a few words with the Knight, remained to see the disposal of the men, while Sir Reginald himself entered the hall with his wife, son and brother. Eustace did not long remain there: he found that Reginald and Eleanor had much to say to each other, and his curiosity and interest were, besides, greatly excited by the novelty of the scene presented by the castle court, so different from its usual peaceful monotony. The men were unsaddling their horses, rubbing them down, walking them about, or removing the stains of dust and mud from their own armour, while others were exchanging greetings with the villagers, who were gathering in joyous parties round such of the newly arrived as were natives of the place.

In the midst stood the strange Squire, superintending a horse-boy who was rubbing down the Knight's tall war-horse, and at the same time ordering, giving directions, answering inquiries, or granting permission to the men to return home

5

with their relations. Ralph Penrose was near, his countenance, as Eustace could plainly perceive, expressing little satisfaction at finding another authority in the court of Lynwood Keep; the references to himself short, brief, and rapid, and only made when ignorance of the locality compelled the stranger to apply for information. The French accent and occasional French phrases with which the Squire spoke, made him contract his brow more and more, and at last, just as Eustace came up, he walked slowly away, grumbling to himself, "Well, have it e'en your own way, I am too old for your gay French fashions. It was not so in Humfrey Harwood's time, when— But the world has gone after the French now! Sir Reginald has brought home as many Gascon thieves as kindly Englishmen!"

Eustace listened for a moment to his mutterings, but without answering them, and coming within a few steps of the stranger, stood waiting to offer him any courtesy in his power, though at the same time he felt abashed by the consciousness of his inferiority in accomplishments and experience.

It was the Squire who was the first to speak. "So this is Sir Reginald's old Keep! A fine old fortalice—would stand at least a fortnight's siege. Ha! Is not yonder a weak point? I would undertake to scale that tower, so the battering-rams made a diversion on the other side."

"I trust it will never be tried," said Eustace.

"It would be as fair a feat of arms as ever you beheld! But I crave your pardon," added he, displaying his white teeth with a merry laugh; "the state of my own land has taught me to look on every castle with eyes for attack and defence, and your brother tells me I am not behind my countrymen in what you English call gasconades."

"You have seen many sieges and passages of arms?" asked Eustace, looking up in his face with an expression at once puzzled and respectful.

"Since our castle of Albricorte was sacked and burnt by the Count de Bearn, I have seen little else—three stricken fields—two towns stormed—castles more than I can remember."

"Alas!" said Eustace, "I have seen nothing but the muster of arms at Taunton!"

D'Aubricour laughed. "Look not downcast on it," said he; "you have time before you and one year at Bordeaux is worth four elsewhere. But I forget, you are the young clerk; and yet that scarcely accords with that bright eye of yours, and the weapon at your side."

"They spoke once of making me a clerk," said Eustace; "but I hope to show my brother that I am fit for his own way of life. Sir Squire, do but tell me, do you think I look unfit to sustain the honour of my name?"

"Mere strength is little," said the Squire, "else were that comely giant John Ingram, the best warrior in the army. Nor does height reckon for much; Du Guesclin himself is of the shortest. Nor do you look like the boy over whose weakly timid nature I have heard Sir Reginald lament," he proceeded, surveying him with a critical eye.

Eustace had, in fact, hardly reached the middle height, and was very slender; his limbs were, however, well proportioned, his step firm, and every movement full of activity and grace. His face, shaded with bright chestnut hair, was of a delicate complexion, the features finely moulded, and the usual cast of expression slightly thoughtful; but there was frequently, and especially at this moment, a bright kindling light in the dark blue eyes, which changed the whole countenance from the grave and refined look of the young scholar to the bold ardent glance of the warrior.

"A cavalier, every inch of you!" cried d'Aubricour, striking Eustace on the shoulder as he concluded his inspection. "I'll have the training of you, my *gentil damoiseau*, and see if I do not make you as *preux a chevalier* as the most burly giant of them all. Here, know you this trick?"

He caught up one of the lances which the men had laid aside; Eustace followed his example, and acquitted himself to his satisfaction in one or two chivalrous manoeuvres, till a summons to supper put an end to the sport.

CHAPTER 2

The house of Lynwood had long been famed for loyalty, which had often cost them dear, since their neighbours, the Lords of Clarenham, never failed to take advantage of the ascendency of the popular party, and make encroachments on their privileges and possessions.

Thus when Sir Hugo Lynwood, the old Crusader, was made prisoner by Simon de Montfort's party at Lewes, he was treated with great severity, in order to obtain from him a recognition of the feudal superiority of the Clarenhams; and though the success of the royal party at Evesham occasioned his liberation, his possessions were greatly diminished. Nor had the turmoils of the reign of Edward II. failed to leave their traces on the fortunes of the Lynwoods. Sir Henry, father of the present Knight, was a staunch adherent of the unfortunate monarch, and even joined the hapless Edmund, Earl of Kent, in the rising in which that Prince was entrapped after the murder of his brother. On this occasion, it was only Sir Henry's hasty flight that preserved his life, and his lands were granted to the Baron Simon de Clarenham by the young Edward III., then under the dominion of his mother Isabel, and Roger Mortimer; but when at length the King had freed himself from their trammels, the whole county of Somerset rose to expel the intruders from Lynwood Keep, and reinstate its true master. Nor did Simon de Clarenham make much resistance, for well knowing that an appeal to the King would occasion and instant revocation of the grant, he judged it advisable to allow it to sleep for the present.

Sir Henry Lynwood, therefore, lived and died unmolested. His eldest son, Reginald, was early sent to the Royal Camp, where he soon distinguished himself, and gained the favour and friendship of the gallant Prince of Wales. The feud with the Clarenhams seemed to be completely extinguished, when Reginald, chiefly by the influence of the Prince, succeeded in obtaining the hand of a lady of that family, the daughter of a brave Knight slain in the wars in Brittany.

Since this time, both the Baron de Clarenham and his son, Sir Fulk, had been on good terms with the Knight of Lynwood, and the connection had been drawn still closer by the Baron's second marriage with the Lady Muriel de la Poer, a near relative of Sir Reginald's mother. Many a time had Dame Eleanor Lynwood ridden to Clarenham castle, under the escort of her young brother-in-law, to whom such a change from the lonely old Keep afforded no small delight.

Eustace, the only one of Sir Henry's younger children who survived the rough nursing or the over-nursing, whichever it might be, that thinned in former days the families of nobles and gentleman, might as well, in the opinion of almost all, have rested beneath a quaint little image of his infant figure, in brass, in the vaults of the little Norman chapel; for he was a puny, ailing child, apt to scandalize his father and brother, and their warlike retainers, by being scared at the dazzling helm and nodding crest, and preferring the seat at this mother's feet, the fairy tale of the old nurse, the song of the minstrel, or the book of the Priest, to horse and hound, or even to the sight of the martial sports of the tilt-yard.

The last five years had, however, wrought a great change in him; he began to outgrow the delicacy of his constitution, and with it, to shake off his timidity of disposition. A diligent perusal of the romances of chivalry filled him with emulation, and he had applied himself ardently to all knightly exercises, looking with great eagerness to the time when he might appear in the Prince's court. He had invested it with all the glory of the Round Table and of the Paladins; and though he knew he must not look for Merlin or the Siege Perilous, the men themselves were in his fancy Rolands and Tristrems, and he scarcely dared to hope he could ever be fit to make one of them, with all his diligent attention to old Ralph's instructions.

Some of Ralph's manoeuvres were indeed rather antiquated, and afforded much amusement to Gaston d'Aubricour, who was never weary of teasing the old seneschal with descriptions of the changes in the fashion of weapons, tourneys, and machines, and especially delighted in histories of the marvellous effects of gunpowder. Ralph would shake his head, vow that it would soon put an end to all true chivalry, and walk off to furbish his favourite cross-bow, with many a murmured reflection on the folly of quitting good old plans, and especially on that of his master, who must needs bring home a gibing Gascon, when honest English Squires were not scarce.

Very different was the state of the old Keep of Lynwood from the quiet, almost deserted condition, in which it had been left so long, now that the Knight had again taken his wonted place amongst the gentry of the county. Entertainments were exchanged with his neighbours, hunting and hawking matches, and all the sports of the tilt-yard, followed each other in quick succession, and the summer passed merrily away. Merrily, that is to say, with Sir Reginald, whose stirring life in camp and court had left him but few and short intervals for enjoying his home and the society of his wife; with Eleanor, who, relieved from long anxiety, began to recover the spirits and health which had nearly failed her; and with Eustace, to whom the arrival of his brother and his followers brought a continued course of novelty and delight; but less joyously with the Knight's followers, who regretted more and more the gay court of Bordeaux, and grew impatient at the prospect of spending a tedious winter in a peaceful English castle.

Their anticipation of weariness, and the contrary expectations of Sir Reginald, were destined to be equally disappointed: for two months had not passed since his return before a summons arrived, or, more properly speaking, an invitation to the trusty and well-beloved Sir Reginald Lynwood to join the forces which the Duke of Lancaster was assembling at Southampton, the Prince of Wales having promised to assist King Pedro of Castile in recovering the kingdom from which he had been driven by his brother Enrique of Trastamare.

Sir Reginald could not do otherwise than prepare with alacrity to obey the call of his beloved Prince, though he marvelled that Edward should draw his sword in the cause of such a monster of cruelty, and he was more reluctant than ever before to leave his home. He even promised his sorrowful Eleanor that this should be the last time he would leave her. "I will but bestow Eustace in some honourable household, where he may be trained in knightly lore—that of Chandos, perchance, or some other of the leaders who hold the good old strict rule; find good masters for my honest men-at-arms; break one more lance with Du Guesclin; and take to rule my vassals, till my fields, and be the honest old country Knight my father was before me. Said I well, Dame Eleanor?"

Eleanor smiled, but the next moment sighed and drooped her head, while a tear fell on the blue silk with which she was embroidering the crosslet on his pennon. Sir Reginald might have said somewhat to cheer her, but at that instant little Arthur darted into the hall with news that the armourer was come from Taunton, with two mules, loaded with a store of goodly helmets, swords, and corselets, which he was displaying in the court.

The Knight immediately walked forth into the court, where all had been activity and eagerness ever since the arrival of the summons, the smith hammering ceaselessly in his forge, yet without fulfilling half the order continually shouted in his ears; Gaston d'Aubricour and Ralph Penrose directing from morning to night, in contradiction of each other, the one always laughing, the other always grumbling; the men-at-arms and retainers some obeying orders, others being scolded, the steel clanging, hammers ringing without intermission. Most of the party, such at least as could leave their employment without a sharp reprimand from one or the other of the contending authorities, the Seneschal and the Squire, were gathered round the steps, where the armourer was displaying, with many an encomium, his bundles of lances, his real Toledo blades, and his helmets of the choicest fashion. Gaston d'Aubricour and Ralph were disputing respecting a certain suit of armour, which the latter disapproved, because it had no guards for the knees, while the former contended that the only use for such protections was to disable a man from walking, and nearly from standing when once unhorsed.

"In my day, Master d'Aubricour, it was not the custom for a brave man-at-arms to look to being unhorsed; but times are changed."

"Ay, that they are, Master Penrose, for in our day we do not give ourselves over the moment we are down, and lie closed up in our shells like great land tortoises turned on their backs, waiting till some one is good enough to find his way through our shell with the *misericorde*."

"Peace, peace, Gaston," said the Knight. "If we acquit ourselves as well as our fathers, we shall have little to be ashamed of. What think you of this man's gear?"

9

"That I could pick up a better suit for half the price at old Battista, the Lombard's at Bordeaux; nevertheless, since young Eustace would be the show of the camp if he appeared there provided in Ralph's fashion, it may be as well to see whether there be any reasonableness in this old knave."

Before the question was decided, the trampling of horses was heard, and there rode into the court an elderly man, whose dress and bearing showed him to be of consideration, accompanied by a youth of eighteen or nineteen, and attended by two servants. Sir Reginald and his brother immediately stepped forward to receive them.

"Sir Philip Ashton," said the former, "how is it with you? This is friendly in you to come and bid us farewell."

"I grieve that it should be farewell, Sir Reginald," said the old Knight, dismounting whilst Eustace held his stirrup; "our country can ill spare such men as you. Thanks, my young friend Eustace. See, Leonard, what good training will do for an Esquire; Eustace has already caught that air and courteous demeanour that cannot be learnt here among us poor Knights of Somerset."

This was to his son, who, with a short abrupt reply to the good-natured greeting of Sir Reginald, had scrambled down from his saddle, and stood fixing his large gray eyes upon Gaston, whose tall active figure and lively dark countenance seemed to afford him an inexhaustible subject of study. The Squire was presented by name to Sir Philip, received a polite compliment, and replying with a bow, turned to the youth with the ready courtesy of one willing to relieve the shyness of an awkward stranger. "We were but now discussing the merit between damasked steel and chain mail, what opinion do you bring to aid us?" A renewed stare, an inarticulate muttering, and Master Leonard turned away and almost hid his face in the mane of his horse, whilst his father attempted to make up for his incivility by a whole torrent of opinions, to which Gaston listened with the outward submission due from a Squire, but with frequent glances, accompanied by a tendency to elevate shoulder or eyebrow, which Eustace understood full well to convey that the old gentleman knew nothing whatever on the subject.

This concluded, Sir Philip went to pay his respects to the Lady of Lynwood, and then, as the hour of noon had arrived, all partook of the meal, which was served in the hall, the Squires waiting on the Knights and the Lady before themselves sitting down to table.

It was the influence of dinner that first unchained the silent tongue of Leonard Ashton, when he found himself seated next to his old acquaintance, Eustace Lynwood, out of hearing of those whose presence inspired him with shyness, and the clatter of knives and trenchers drowning his voice.

"So your brother has let you bear sword after all. How like you the trade? Better than poring over crabbed parchments, I trow. But guess you why we are here to-day? My father says that I must take service with some honourable Knight, and see somewhat of the world. He spoke long of the Lord de Clarenham, because his favour would be well in the county; but at last he has fixed on your brother, because he may do somewhat for me with the Prince."

"Then you are going with us to Bordeaux?" exclaimed Eustace, eagerly.

10

"Ay, truly."

"Nay, but that is a right joyful hearing!" said Eustace. "Old friends should be brethren in arms."

"But, Eustace," said young Ashton, lowering his voice to a confidential whisper, "I like not that outlandish Squire, so tall and black. Men say he is a Moor—a worshipper of Mahound."

Eustace laughed heartily at this report, and assured his friend that, though he had heard his brother often give his Squire in jest his *nom de guerre* of *Gaston le Maure*, yet d'Aubricour was a gallant gentleman of Gascony. But still Leonard was not satisfied. "Had ever man born in Christian land such flashing black eyes and white teeth? And is not he horribly fierce and strict?"

"Never was man of kinder heart and blither temper."

"Then you think that he will not be sharp with us? 'More straight in your saddle!' 'lance lower!' 'head higher,' that is what has been ringing in my ears from morning till night of late, sometimes enforced by a sharp blow on the shoulders. Is it not so with you?"

"Oh, old Penrose took all that trouble off their hands long ago. Gaston is the gentlest of tutors compared with him."

"I hope so!" sighed Leonard; "my very bones ache with the tutoring I get from my father at home. And, Eustace, resolve me this—"

"Hush, do not you see that Father Cyril is about to pronounce the Grace—. There—now must I go and serve your father with the grace-cup, but I will be with you anon."

Leonard put his elbow on the table, mumbling to himself, "And these of Eustace's be the courtly manners my father would have me learn; they cost a great deal too much trouble!"

The meal over, Eustace took Leonard into the court to visit the horses and inspect the new armour. They were joined by Gaston, who took upon himself to reply to the question which Leonard wished to have resolved, namely, what they were to do in Castile, by persuading him to believe that Enrique of Trastamare was a giant twenty feet high, who rode a griffin of proportionate dimensions, and led an army whose heads grew under their shoulders.

In the meantime, Sir Philip Ashton was, with many polite speeches, entering upon the business of his visit, which was to request Sir Reginald to admit his son into his train as an Esquire. The Knight of Lynwood, though not very desirous of this addition to his followers, could not well refuse him, in consideration of the alliance which had long subsisted between the two houses; but he mentioned his own purpose of quitting the Prince's court as soon as the present expedition should be concluded.

"That," said Sir Philip, softly, "will scarce be likely. Such Knights as Sir Reginald Lynwood are not so easily allowed to hide themselves in obscurity. The Prince of Wales knows too well the value of his right-hand counsellor."

"Nay, Sir Philip," said Sir Reginald, laughing, "that is rather too fine a term for a rough soldier, who never was called into counsel at all, except for the arraying a battle. It would take far sharper wits than mine, or, indeed, I suspect, than any that

11

we have at Bordeaux, to meet the wiles of Charles of France. No, unless the Royal Banner be abroad in the field, you may look to see me here before another year is out."

"I shall hope it may be otherwise, for my boy's sake," said Sir Philip. "But be that as it may, his fame will be secured by his going forth for the first time with such a leader as yourself. The example and friendship of your brother will also be of the utmost service. Your chief Squire too—so perfect in all chivalrous training, and a foreigner—who better could be found to train a poor Somersetshire clown for the Prince's Gascon court?"

"Why, for that matter," interrupted Sir Reginald, whose patience would seldom serve his to the end of one of his neighbour's harangues, "it may be honest to tell you that though Gaston is a kindly-tempered fellow, and of right knightly bearing, his life has been none of the most steady. I took up with him a couple of years since, when poor old Humfrey Harwood was slain at Auray, and I knew not where to turn for a Squire. Save for a few wild freaks now and then, he has done right well, though I sometimes marvelled at his choosing to endure my strict household. He obeys my orders, and has made himself well liked by the men, and I willingly trust Eustace with him, since the boy is of a grave clerkly sort of turn, and under my own eye; but it is for you to do as you will with your son."

"Is he of honourable birth?" asked Sir Philip.

"At least he bears coat armour," answered Reginald. "His shield is *gules*, a wolf *passant*, *or*, and I have heard strange tales of his father, Beranger d'Aubricour, the Black Wolf of the Pyrenees, as he was called, one of the robber noblesse of the Navarrese border; but I have little time for such matters, and they do not dwell in my mind. If I find a man does his duty in my service, I care not whence he comes, nor what his forefathers may have been. I listen to no such idle tales; but I thought it best to warn you that I answer not for all the comrades your son may find in my troop."

"Many thanks, noble Sir Reginald; under such care as yours he cannot fail to prosper; I am secure of his welfare in your hands. One word more, Sir Reginald, I pray you. You are all-powerful with Prince Edward. My poor boy's advancement is in your hand. One word in his favour to the Prince—a hint of the following I could send his pennon—"

"Sir Philip," said Reginald, "you overrate my influence, and underrate the Prince's judgment, if you imagine aught save personal merit would weigh with him. Your son shall have every opportunity of deserving his notice, but whether it be favourable or not must depend on himself. If you desire more, you must not seek it of me."

Sir Philip protested that this was all he wished, and after reiterating his thanks, took his leave, promising that Leonard should be at Lynwood Keep on the next Monday, the day fixed for Sir Reginald's departure.

12

CHAPTER III

The morning of departure arrived. The men-at-arms were drawn up in the court like so many statues of steel; Leonard Ashton sat on horseback, his eyes fixed on the door; Gaston d'Aubricour, wrapped in his gay mantle, stood caressing his Arab steed Brigliador, and telling him they should soon exchange the chilly fogs of England for the bright sun of Gascony; Ralph Penrose held his master's horse, and a black powerful charger was prepared for Eustace, but still the brothers tarried.

"My Eleanor, this should not be!" said Reginald as his wife clung to him weeping. "Keep a good heart. 'Tis not for long. Take heed of your dealings with cousin Fulk. She knows not what I say. Father Cyril, keep guard over her and my boy, in case I should meet with any mishap."

"I will, assuredly, my son," said the Chaplain, "but it is little that a poor Priest like me can do. I would that grant to the Clarenhams were repealed."

"That were soon done," said Reginald, "but it is no time for a loyal vassal to complain of grievances when his liege lord has summoned him to the field. That were to make the King's need be his law. No! no! Watch over her, good father, she is weak and tender. Look up, sweet heart, give me one cheerful wish to speed me on my journey. No? She has swooned. Eleanor! my wife—"

"Begone, begone, my son," said Father Cyril, "it will be the better for her."

"It may be," said Reginald, "yet to leave her thus— Here, nurse, support her, tend her well. Give her my tenderest greetings. Arthur, be duteous to her; talk to her of our return; farewell, my boy, and blessings on you. Eustace, mount."

Sir Reginald, sighing heavily, swung himself into the saddle; Eustace waited a moment longer. "Good Father, this was to have been in poor Eleanor's charge. It is the token, you know for whom."

"It shall reach her, my son."

"You will send me a letter whenever you can?"

"Truly, I will; and I would have you read and write, especially in Latin, when you have the chance—good gifts should not be buried. Bethink you, too, that you will not have the same excuse for sin as the rude ignorant men you will meet."

"Eustace!" hastily called Reginald, and with a hurried farewell to all around, the young Squire sprang on horseback, and the troop rode across the drawbridge. They halted on the mound beyond; Sir Reginald shook his pennon, till the long white swallow tails streamed on the wind, then placed it in the hands of Eustace, and saying, "On, Lances of Lynwood! In the name of God, St. George, and King Edward, do your devoir;" he spurred his horse forward, as if only desirous to be out of sight of his own turrets, and forget the parting, the pain of which still heaved his breast and dimmed his eye.

A few days brought the troop to Southampton, where John of Gaunt was collecting his armament, and with it they embarked, crossed to St. Malo, and thence proceeded to Bordeaux, but there found that the Prince of Wales had already set forth, and was waiting for his brother at Dax.

Advancing immediately, at the end of three days they came in sight of the

13

forces encamped around that town. Glorious was the scene before them, the green plain covered in every direction with white tents, surmounted with the banners or pennons of their masters, the broad red Cross of St. George waving proudly in the midst, and beside it the royal Lions and Castles of the two Spanish monarchies. To the south, the snowy peaks of the Pyrenees began to gleam white like clouds against the sky, and the gray sea-line to the west closed the horizon. Eustace drew his rein, and gazed in silent admiration, and Gaston, riding by his side, pointed out the several bearings and devices which, to the warrior of that day, spoke as plainly (often more so) as written words. "See yonder, the tent of my brave countryman, the Captal de Buch, close to that of the Prince, as is ever his wont. No doubt he is willing to wipe away the memory of his capture at Auray. There, to the left, *gules* and *argent*, per *pale*, is the pennon of the stout old Englishman, Chandos. Ha! I see the old Free Companions are here with Sir Hugh Calverly! Why, 'twas but the other day they were starting to set this very Don Enrique on the throne as blithely as they now go to drive him from his."

While Gaston spoke, the sound of horses' feet approached rapidly from another quarter, and a small party came in sight, the foremost of whom checked his bridle, as, at Reginald's signal, his Lances halted and drew respectfully aside. He was a man about thirty-six years of age, and looking even younger, from the remarkable fairness and delicacy of his complexion. The perfect regularity of his noble features, together with the commanding, yet gentle expression of his clear light blue eyes, would, even without the white ostrich feather in his black velvet cap, have enabled Eustace to recognize in him the flower of chivalry, Edward, Prince of Wales.

"Welcome, my trusty Reginald!" exclaimed he. "I knew that the Lances of Lynwood would not be absent where knightly work is to be done. Is my brother John arrived?"

"Yes, my Lord," replied Reginald; "I parted from him but now as he rode to the castle, while I came to seek where to bestow my knaves."

"I know you of old for a prudent man," said the Prince, smiling; "the Provost Marshal hath no acquaintance with that gallant little band. Methinks I see there a fair face like enough to yours to belong to another loyal Lynwood."

"I could wish it were a little browner and more manly, my Lord," said Reginald. "It is my brother Eustace, who has been suffered (I take shame to myself for it) to tarry at home as my Lady's page, till he looks as white as my Lady herself."

"We will soon find a cure for that in the sun of Castile," said Edward. "You are well provided with Squires. The men of Somerset know where good training is to be found for their sons."

"This, my Lord, is the son of Sir Philip Ashton, a loyal Knight of our country."

"He is welcome," said the Prince. "We have work for all. Let me see you this evening at supper in my tent."

"Well, Eustace, what sayest thou?" said Gaston, as the Prince rode on.

"A Prince to dream of, a Prince for whom to give a thousand lives!" said Eustace.

"And that was the Prince of Wales!" said Leonard. "Why, he spoke just like any

14

other man."

The two tents of the Lances of Lynwood having been erected, and all arrangements made, the Knights and Squires set out for the Prince's pavilion, the white curtains of which were conspicuous in the centre of the camp. Within, it was completely lined with silk, embroidered with the various devices of the Prince: the lions of England—the lilies of France—the Bohemian ostrich-plume, with its humble motto, the white rose, not yet an emblem of discord—the blue garter and the red cross, all in gorgeous combination—a fitting background, as it were, on which to display the chivalrous groups seen in relief against it.

At the upper end was placed a long table for the Prince and his guests, and here Sir Reginald took his seat, with many a hearty welcome from his friends and companions in arms, while Gaston led his comrades to the lower end, where Squires and pages were waiting for the provisions brought in by the servants, which they were to carry to their Knights. Gaston was soon engaged in conversation with his acquaintance, to some of whom he introduced Eustace and Leonard, but the former found far more interesting occupation in gazing on the company seated at the upper table.

The Black Prince himself occupied the centre, his brother John at his left hand, and at his right, a person whom both this post of honour and the blazonry of his surcoat marked out as the dethroned King of Castile. Pedro the Cruel had not, however, the forbidding countenance which imagination would ascribe to him; his features were of the fair and noble type of the old royal Gothic race of Spain; he had a profusion of flaxen hair, and large blue eyes, rather too prominent, and but for his receding forehead, and the expression of his lips, he would have been a handsome man of princely mien. Something, too, there was of fear, something of a scowl; he seemed to shrink from the open and manly demeanour of Edward, and to turn with greater ease to converse with John, who, less lofty in character than his brother, better suited his nature.

There, too, Eustace beheld the stalwart form and rugged features of Sir John Chandos; the slender figure and dark sparkling southern face of the Captal de Buch; the rough joyous boon-companion visage of Sir Hugh Calverly, the free-booting warrior; the youthful form of the young step-son of the Prince, Lord Thomas Holland; the rude features of the Breton Knight, Sir Oliver de Clisson, soon to be the bitterest foe of the standard beneath which he was now fighting. Many were there whose renown had charmed the ears of the young Squire of Lynwood Keep, and he looked on the scene with the eagerness with which he would have watched some favourite romance suddenly done into life and action.

"Eustace! What, Eustace, in a trance?" said d'Aubricour. "Waken, and carry this trencher of beef to your brother. Best that you should do it," he added in a low voice, taking up a flask of wine, "and save our comrade from at once making himself a laughing-stock."

The discontented glance with which Leonard's eyes followed his fellow Squires, did not pass unobserved by a person with whom d'Aubricour had exchanged a few words, a squarely-made, dark-visaged man, with a thick black beard, and a huge scar which had obliterated one eye; his equipment was that of a Squire, but

15

instead of, like others of the same degree, attending on the guests at the upper table, he sat carelessly sideways on the bench, with one elbow on the board.

"You gaze after that trencher as if you wished your turn was come," said he, in a patois of English and French, which Leonard could easily understand, although he had always turned a deaf ear to Gaston's attempts to instruct him in the latter language. However, a grunt was his only reply.

"Or," pursued the Squire, "have you any fancy for carrying it yourself? I, for my part, think we are well quit of the trouble."

"Why, ay," said Leonard, "but I trow I have as much right to serve at the Prince's table as dainty Master Eustace. My father had never put me under Sir Reginald's charge, had he deemed I should be kept here among the serving-men."

"Sir Reginald? Which Sir Reginald has the honour of your service?" asked the Squire, to whom Leonard's broad Somersetshire dialect seemed to present few difficulties.

"Sir Reginald Lynwood, he with the curled brown locks, next to that stern-looking old fellow with the gray hair."

"Ay, I know him of old. Him whom the Duke of Lancaster is pledging—a proud, strict Englishman—as rigid a service as any in the camp."

"I should think so!" said Leonard. "Up in the morn hours before the sun, to mass like a choir of novices, to clean our own arms and the Knight's, like so many horse-boys, and if there be but a speck of rust, or a sword-belt half a finger's length awry—"

"Ay, ay, I once had a fortnight's service with a Knight of that stamp, but a fortnight was enough for me, I promise you. And yet Gaston le Maure chooses to stay with him rather than lead a merry life with Sir Perduccas d'Albret, with all to gain, and nought to lose! A different life from the days he and I spent together of old."

"Gaston d'Aubricour is as sharp as the Knight himself," said Leonard, "and gibes me without ceasing; but yet I could bear it all, were it not for seeing Eustace, the clerk, preferred to me, as if I were not heir to more acres than he can ever count crowns."

"What may then be your name, fair youth, and your inheritance?" demanded the one-eyed Squire, "for your coat of arms is new in the camp."

"My name is Leonard Ashton; my father—" but Leonard's speech was cut short by a Squire who stumbled over his outstretched foot. Both parties burst into angry exclamations, Leonard's new acquaintance taking his part. Men looked up, and serious consequences might have ensued, had not Gaston hastened to the spot. "Shame on you, young malapert," said he to his hopeful pupil. "Cannot I leave you one moment unwatched, but you must be brawling in the Prince's own presence? Here, bear this bread to Sir Reginald instantly, and leave me to make your peace. Master Clifford," added he, as Leonard shuffled away, "'tis an uncouth slip whom Sir Reginald Lynwood has undertaken to mould into form, and if he is visited as he deserves for each piece of discourtesy, his life will not be long enough for amendment, so I must e'en beg you to take my apology."

"Most readily, Master d'Aubricour," replied Clifford; "there would not have been

16

the least offence had the youth only possessed a civil tongue."

"Is not he the son of one of your wealthy Englishmen?" asked the one-eyed Squire, carelessly.

"Ha! Why should you think so?" said Gaston, turning sharply; "because he shows so much good nurture?"

"Because his brains are grown fat with devouring his father's beeves, fare on which you seem to thrive, le Maure," said the one-eyed, "though you were not wont to like English beef and English discipline better than Gascon wine and Gascon freedom. I begin to think that the cub of the Black Wolf of the Pyrenees is settling down into a tame English house-dog."

"He has teeth and claws at your service," replied Gaston.

"Ay?" said the Squire interrogatively; then, changing his tone, "But tell me honestly, Gaston, repent you not of having taken service with gallant Sir Perduccas?"

"Why, you have left him yourself."

"Yes, because we had sharp words on the spoil of a Navarrese village. My present leader, Sir William Felton, is as free and easy as d'Albret, or Aymerigot Marcel himself. And is not yon ungainly varlet the hope of some rich English house?"

"I must see their hopes meet with no downfall," said Gaston, walking away, and muttering to himself. "A plague upon it! To train two boys is more than I bargained for, and over and above to hinder this wiseacre Ashton from ruining himself, or being ruined by *le Borgne Basque*! What brought him here? I thought he was safe in Castile with the Free Companions. I would let the oaf take his course, for a wilful wrong-headed fool, but that it would scarce be doing good service to Sir Reginald."

The Knights had nearly finished their meal, and the Squires having served them with wine, returned to their own table, now freshly supplied with meat, which the yeomen in their turn carved for them. Gaston kept Leonard under his own eye till the party broke up.

On the way to the tent, he began to take him to task. "A proper commencement! Did you take the Prince's pavilion for one of your own island hostels, where men may freely brawl and use their fists without fear of aught save the parish constable?"

"What business had he to tread on my foot?" growled Leonard.

"What business had your foot there? Was not your office, as I told you, to stand ready to hand me whatever I might call for?"

"I was speaking a few words to another gentleman."

"The fewer words you speak to *le Borgne Basque* the better, unless you think it is Sir Reginald's pleasure that you should be instructed in all the dicing and drinking in this camp, and unless you wish that the crowns with which your father stored your pouch should jingle in his pockets. It is well for you the Knight marked you not."

"You held long enough parley with him yourself," said the refractory pupil.

"Look you, Master Leonard Ashton, I do not presume to offer myself as an

17

example to you save, perhaps, in the matter of sitting a steed, or handing a wine-cup. I have no purse to lose, and I have wit to keep it if I had, or at least," as a recollection crossed him, "if I lost it, it should be to please myself, and not *le Borgne Basque*; above all, my name and fame are made, and yours—"

"What would you say of mine?" said Leonard, with sulky indignation. "The heir of Ashton is not to be evened to a wandering landless foreigner."

"It is not in sight of these mountain peaks," said Gaston, contemptuously, "that I am to be called a foreigner; and as to being landless, if I chose to take my stand on the old tower of Albricorte, and call myself Lord of the whole hill-side, I should like to see who would gainsay me. For name, I suspect you will find that many a man has trembled at the sound of Beranger d'Albricorte, to whom Ashton would be but that of an English clown. Moreover, in this camp I would have you to know that the question is, not who has the broadest lands, but who has the strongest arm. And, sir Squire, if you are not above listening to a piece of friendly counsel, to brag of those acres of yours is the surest way to attract spoilers. I had rather a dozen time trust Eustace in such company than you, not only because he has more wit, but because he has less coin."

"Who is this man? What is his name?" asked Eustace.

"*Le Borgne Basque*, I know no other," said Gaston. "We reck little of names here, especially when it may be convenient to have them forgotten. He is a Free Companion, a *routier*, brave enough, but more ready at the sack than the assault, and loving best to plunder, waste, and plunder again, or else to fleece such sheep as our friend here."

"How could such a man gain entrance to the Prince's pavilion?"

"Stout hearts and strong arms find entrance in most places," said Gaston; "but, as you saw, he durst not appear at the upper table."

The next morning the army began their march to the Pyrenees. They halted for some days at the foot of the hills, whilst negotiations were passing between the Black Prince and Charles the Bad, King of Navarre, who might easily have prevented their entrance into the Peninsula by refusing a passage through his mountain fastnesses.

When the permission was granted, they advanced with considerable danger and difficulty. The rugged paths were covered with snow and ice, which made them doubly perilous for the horses, and but for Gaston's familiarity with his native hills, Sir Reginald declared that he could never have brought his little troop across them in safety.

At length they emerged through the celebrated Pass of Roncesvalles, where Eustace in imagination listened to the echoes of the dying blast of Roland. On the following evening he had the delight of reading his history in the veritable pages of Archbishop Turpin, which precious work he found in the possession of Brother Waleran, a lay-friar, in the employment of Sir John Froissart the chronicler, who had sent him with the army as a reporter of the events of the campaign. This new acquaintance gave very little satisfaction to Sir Reginald, who was almost ready to despair of Eustace's courage and manhood when he found he had "gone back to his books," and manifested, if not so much serious

18

displeasure, yet even more annoyance, on this occasion, than when, shortly after, he found that Leonard Ashton spent every moment at his own disposal in the company of *le Borgne Basque*. That worthy, meeting the young gentleman, had easily persuaded him that Gaston's cautions only proceeded from fears of stories that might with too much truth be told against himself, and by skilful flatteries of the young Englishman's self-importance, and sympathy with his impatience of the strict rule of the Knight of Lynwood, succeeded in establishing over him great influence.

So fared it with the two young Squires, whilst the army began to enter the dominions of the King of Castile. Here a want of provisions was severely felt, for such was the hatred borne to Pedro the Cruel, that every inhabitant of the country fled at his approach, carrying off, or destroying, all that could be used as food. It was the intention of Bertrand du Guesclin, the ally of Enrique of Trastamare, to remain quietly in his camp of Navaretta, and allow hunger to do its work with the invading force, but this prudent plan was prevented by the folly of Don Tello, brother of Enrique, who, accusing Bertrand of cowardice, so stung his fiery spirit that he resolved on instant combat, though knowing how little dependence could be placed on his Spanish allies.

The challenge of the Prince of Wales was therefore accepted; and never were tidings more welcome than these to the half-famished army, encamped upon the banks of the Ebro, on the same ground on which, in after years, English valour was once more to turn to flight a usurping King of Spain.

CHAPTER IV

The moon was at her height, and shone full into the half-opened tent of Sir Reginald Lynwood. At the further end, quite in darkness, the Knight, bare-headed, and rosary in hand, knelt before the dark-robed figure of a confessor, while at a short distance lay, on a couch of deer-skins, the sleeping Leonard Ashton. Before the looped-up curtain that formed the door was Gaston d'Aubricour, on one knee, close to a huge torch of pine-wood fixed in the earth, examining by its flaring smoky light into the state of his master's armour, proving every joint with a small hammer. Near him, Eustace, with the help of John Ingram, the stalwart yeoman, was fastening his charge, the pennon, to a mighty lance of the toughest ash-wood, and often looking forth on the white tents on which the moonbeams shed their pale, tranquil light. There was much to impress a mind like his, in the scene before him: the unearthly moonlight, the few glimmering stars, the sky—whose southern clearness and brightness were, to his unaccustomed eye, doubly wonderful—the constant though subdued sounds in the camp, the murmur of the river, and,—far away in the dark expanse of night, the sparkling of a multitude of lights, which marked the encampment of the enemy. There was a strange calm awe upon his spirit. He spoke in a low voice, and Gaston's careless light-hearted tones fell on his ear as something uncongenial; but his eye glanced brightly, his step was free and bold, as he felt that this was the day that must silence every irritating doubt of his possessing a warrior-spirit.

19

The first red streak of dawn was beginning to glow in the eastern sky, when the note of a bugle rang out from the Prince's tent and was responded to by hundreds of other horns. That instant the quiet slumbering camp awoke, the space in front of every tent was filled with busy men, arming themselves, or saddling their horses. Gaston and Eustace, already fully equipped, assisted Sir Reginald to arm; Leonard was roused, and began to fasten on his armour; the men-at-arms came forth from their tent, and the horses were saddled and bridled; "And now," called Sir Reginald, "bring our last loaf, John Ingram. Keep none back. By this day's eve we shall have abundance, or else no further need."

The hard dry barley-bread was shared in scanty, but equal measure, and scarcely had it been devoured, before a second bugle blast, pealing through the camp, caused each mail-clad warrior to close his visor, and spring into the open plain, where, according to previous orders, they arrayed themselves in two divisions, the first commanded by the Duke of Lancaster and Sir John Chandos, the second by Prince Edward and Don Pedro.

After a pause, employed in marshalling the different bands, the host advanced at an even pace, the rising sun glancing on their armour, and revealing the multitude of waving crests, and streamers fluttering from the points of the lances, like the wings of gorgeous insects. Presently a wall of glittering armour was seen advancing to meet them, with the same brilliant display. It might have seemed some mighty tournament that was there arrayed, as the two armies stood confronting each other, rather than a stern battle for the possession of a kingdom; and well might old Froissart declare, "It was a pleasure to see such hosts."

But it would be presumptuous to attempt to embellish a tale after Froissart has once touched it. To him, then, I leave it to tell how the rank of banneret was conferred on the gallant old Chandos, how the Prince prayed aloud for a blessing on his arms, how he gave the signal for the advance, and how the boaster, Tello, fled in the first encounter. The Lances of Lynwood, in the division of the Duke of Lancaster, well and gallantly did their part in the hard struggle with the brave band of French, whose resistance was not overcome till the Black Prince himself brought his reserved troops to the aid of his brother.

With the loss of only one man-at-arms, the Lances of Lynwood had taken several prisoners. It was high noon, and the field was well-nigh cleared of the enemy, when Sir Reginald drew his rein at the top of a steep bank clothed with brushwood, sloping towards the stream of the Zadorra, threw up his visor, wiped his heated brow, and, patting his horse's neck, turned to his brother, saying, "You have seen sharp work in this your first battle-day, Eustace."

"It is a glorious day!" said Eustace. "See how they hurry to the water." And he pointed over the low shrubs to a level space on the bank of the river, where several fugitives, on foot and horseback, were crowding together, and pressing hastily forward.

"Ha!" cried Sir Reginald, "the golden circlet! Henry of Trastamare himself!" and at the same instant he sprang to the ground. "You," said he, "speed round the bushes, meet me at the ford they are making for." This was directed to Gaston, and ere the last words were spoken, both Sir Reginald and Eustace were already beginning to hurry down the bank. Gaston rose to his full height in his stirrups, and, looking over the wood, exclaimed, "The Eagle crest! I must be there. On, Ashton—Ingram, this way—speed, speed, speed!" and with these words threw himself from his horse, and dashed after the two brothers, as they went crashing, in their heavy armour, downwards through the boughs. In less than a minute they were on the level ground, and Sir Reginald rushed forward to intercept Don Enrique, who was almost close to the river. "Yield, yield, Sir King!" he shouted; but at the same moment another Knight on foot threw himself between, raising a huge battle-axe, and crying, "Away, away, Sir; leave me to deal with him!" Enrique turned, entered the river, and safely swam his horse to the other side, whilst his champion was engaged in desperate conflict.

The Knight of Lynwood caught the first blow on his shield, and returned it, but without the slightest effect on his antagonist, who, though short in stature, and clumsily made, seemed to possess gigantic strength. A few moments more, and Reginald had fallen at full length on the grass, while his enemy was pressing on, to secure him as a prisoner, or to seize the pennon which Eustace held. The two Squires stood with lifted swords before their fallen master, but it cost only another of those irresistible strokes to stretch Gaston beside Sir Reginald, and Eustace was left alone to maintain the struggle. A few moments more, and the Lances would come up—but how impossible to hold out! The first blow cleft his shield in two, and though it did not pierce his armour, the shock brought him to his knee, and without the support of the staff of the pennon he would have been on the ground. Still, however, he kept up his defence, using sometimes his sword, and sometimes the staff, to parry the strokes of his assailant; but the strife was too unequal, and faint with violent exertion, as well as dizzied by a stroke which the temper of his helmet had resisted, he felt that all would be over with him in another second, when his sinking energies were revived by the cry of "St. George," close at hand. His enemy relaxing his attack, he sprang to his feet, and that instant found himself enclosed, almost swept away, by a crowd of combatants of inferior degree, as well as his own comrades as Free Lances, all of whose weapons were turned upon his opponent. A sword was lifted over the enemy's head from behind, and would the next moment have descended, but that Eustace sprang up, dashed it aside, cried "Shame!" and grasping the arm of the threatened Knight, exclaimed, "Yield, yield! it is your only hope!"

"Yield? and to thee?" said the Knight; "yet it is well meant. The sword of Arthur himself would be of no avail. Tiphaine was right! It is the fated day. Thou art of gentle birth? I yield me then, rescue or no rescue, the rather that I see thou art a gallant youth. Hark you, fellows, I am a prisoner, so get off with you. Your name, bold youth?"

"Eustace Lynwood, brother to this Knight," said Eustace, raising his visor, and panting for breath.

"You need but a few years to nerve your arm. But rest a while, you are almost spent," said the prisoner, in a kind tone of patronage, as he looked at the youthful face of his captor, which in a second had varied from deep crimson to deadly paleness.

"My brother! my brother!" was all Eustace's answer, as he threw himself on the grass beside Gaston, who, though bleeding fast, had raised his master's head, and freed him from his helmet; but his eyes were still closed, and the wound ghastly, for such had been the force of the blow, that the shoulder was well-nigh severed from the collarbone. "Reginald! O brother, look up!" cried Eustace. "O Gaston, does he live?"

"I have crossed swords with him before," said the prisoner. "I grieve for the mishap." Then, as the soldiers crowded round, he waved them off with a gesture of command, which they instinctively obeyed. "Back, clowns, give him air. And here—one of you—bring some water from the river. There, he shows signs of life."

As he spoke, the clattering of horses' feet was heard—all made way, and there rode along the bank of the river a band of Spaniards, headed by Pedro himself, his sword, from hilt to point, streaming with blood, and his countenance ferocious as that of a tiger. "Where is he?" was his cry; "where is the traitor Enrique? I will send him to join the rest of the brood. Where has he hidden himself?"

The prisoner, who had been assisting to life the wounded man out of the path of the trampling horses, turned round, and replied, with marked emphasis, "King Henry of Castile is, thanks to our Lady, safe on the other side of the Zadorra, to recover his throne another day."

"Du Guesclin himself! Ah, dog!" cried Pedro, his eyes glaring with the malignity of a demon, and raising his bloody weapon to hew down Bertrand du Guesclin, for no other was the prisoner, who stood with folded arms, his dark eyes fixed in calm scorn on the King's face, and his sword and axe lying at his feet.

Eustace was instantly at his side, calling out, "My Lord King, he is my prisoner!"

"Thine!" said Pedro, with an incredulous look. "Leave him to my vengeance, and thou shalt have gold—half my treasury—all thy utmost wishes can reach—"

"I give him up to none but my Lord the Prince of Wales," returned the young Squire, undauntedly.

"Fool and caitiff! out of my path! or learn what it is to oppose the wrath of Kings!" cried Pedro.

Eustace grasped his sword. "Sir King, you must win your way to him through my body."

At this moment one of the attendants whispered, "*El Principe, Senor Rey,*" and, in a few seconds more, the Black Prince, with a few followers, rode towards the spot.

Hastily dismounting, Pedro threw himself on his knees to thank him for the victory; but Edward, leaping from his horse, raised him, saying, "It is not to me, but to the Giver of victories, that you should return thanks;" and Eustace almost shuddered to see him embrace the blood-thirsty monster, who, still intent on his prey, began the next moment, "Here, Senor Prince, is the chief enemy—here is the disturber of kingdoms—Du Guesclin himself—and there stands a traitorous boy of your country, who resolutely refuses to yield him to my just vengeance."

As Pedro spoke, the Prince exchanged with Sir Bertrand the courteous

22

salutation of honourable enemies, and then said, in a quiet, grave tone, "It is not our English custom to take vengeance on prisoners of war."

"My Lord," said Eustace, stepping forward, as the Prince looked towards him, "I deliver the prisoner into your princely hands."

"You have our best thanks, Sir Squire," said the Prince. "You are the young Lynwood, if I remember right. Where is your brother?"

"Alas! my Lord, here he lies, sorely hurt," said Eustace, only anxious to be rid of prisoner and Prince, and to return to Reginald, who by this time had, by the care of Gaston, been recalled to consciousness.

"Is it so? I grieve to hear it!" said Edward, with a face of deep concern, advancing to the wounded Knight, bending over him, and taking his hand, "How fares it with you, my brave Reginald?"

"Poorly enough, my Lord," said the Knight, faintly; "I would I could have taken King Henry—"

"Lament not for that," said the Prince, "but receive my thanks for the prize of scarcely less worth, which I owe to your arms."

"What mean you, my Lord? Not Sir Bertrand du Guesclin; I got nothing from him but my death-blow."

"How is this then?" said Edward; "it was from your young brother that I received him."

"Speak, Eustace!" said Sir Reginald, eagerly, and half raising himself; "Sir Bertrand your prisoner? Fairly and honourably? Is it possible?"

"Fairly and honourably, to that I testify," said Du Guesclin. "He knelt before you, and defended your pennon longer than I ever thought to see one of his years resist that curtal-axe of mine. The *routier* villains burst on us, and were closing upon me, when he turned back the weapon that was over my head, and summoned me to yield, which I did the more willingly that so gallant a youth should have such honour as may be acquired by my capture."

"He has it, noble Bertrand," said Edward. "Kneel down, young Squire. Thy name is Eustace? In the name of God, St. Michael, and St. George, I dub thee Knight. Be faithful, brave and fortunate, as on this day. Arise, Sir Eustace Lynwood."

"Thanks, thanks, my gracious Prince," said Reginald, a light glancing in his fading eyes. "I should die content to see my brother's spurs so well earned."

"Die! Say not so, my faithful Reginald. Speed, Denis, and send hither our own leech! I trust you will live to see your son win his spurs as gallantly!"

"No, my good Lord, I am past the power of leech or surgeon; I feel that this is my death-wound. I am glad it was in your cause. All I desire is your protection for my wife—my boy—my brother—"

"Your brother has earned it already," said Edward. "Your child shall be as my own. But, oh! can nought be done? Hasten the surgeon hither! Cheer thee, Reginald!—look up! O! would that Du Guesclin were free, the battle unfought, so that thou wert but safe, mine own dear brother-in-arms!"

"Where is the Prince?" called a voice from behind. "My Lord, my Lord, if you come not speedily, there will be foul slaughter made among the prisoners by your

23

Spanish butcher—King I would say."

"I come, I come, Chandos," answered Edward. "Fare thee well, my brave Reginald; and you, my new-made Knight, send tidings to my tent how it is with him."

He pressed Reginald's hand, and sighing deeply, mounted his horse, and rode off with Sir John Chandos, leaving the wounded Knight to the care of his own followers.

The stream of blood was flowing fast, life was ebbing away, and Sir Reginald's breath was failing, as Eustace, relieving Gaston from his weight, laid his head on his breast, and laved his brow with water from the river. "You have done gallantly, my brave brother; I did wrong to doubt your spirit. Thanks be to God that I can die in peace, sure that Arthur has in you a true and loving guardian. You are young, Eustace, but my trust in you is firm. You will train him in all Christian and godly ways—"

"It shall be the most sacred charge of my life," said Eustace, scarcely able to speak.

"I know it," said Reginald, and making an effort to raise his voice, he continued, "Bear witness, all of you, that I leave my son in the wardship of the King, and of my brother, Sir Eustace Lynwood. And," added he, earnestly, "beware of Fulk Clarenham. Commend me to my sweet Eleanor; tell her she is the last, as the first in my thoughts." Then, after a pause, "Is Gaston here?"

"Yes, Sir Reginald," said Gaston, leaning over him, and pressing the hand which he feebly raised.

"Gaston, farewell, and thanks to you for your true and loving service. Eustace will find wherewith to recompense you in some sort, in my chest at Bordeaux, and my brave Lances likewise. And, Gaston, go not back to the courses and comrades whence I took you. On the word of a dying man, it will be better for you when you are in this case. Leonard, strive to be a true and brave man, though I may not fulfil your father's trust. Eustace—my eyes grow dim—is this you supporting my head—are these your tears? Weep not for me, brother. Save for my poor Eleanor, I would not have it otherwise. Mercy is sure! Hold up the blessed rood—the sign of grace—you are half a clerk, repeat me some holy psalm or prayer."

Eustace raised the cross hilt of his sword, and with a broken voice, commenced the *Miserere*. Sir Reginald at first followed it with his lips, but soon they ceased to move, his head sank back, his hand fell powerless, and with one long gasping breath his faithful and noble spirit departed. For several moments Eustace silently continued to hold the lifeless form in his arms, then raising the face, he imprinted an earnest kiss on the pale lips, laid the head reverently on the ground, hung over it for a short space, and at last, with an effort, passed his hand over his face, and turned away.

His first look was towards d'Aubricour, who sat resting his head on his hand, his elbow supported on his knee, while with the other hand he dashed away his tears. His countenance was deathly pale, and drops of blood were fast falling from the deep gash in his side. "O Gaston!" exclaimed Eustace, with a feeling of self-reproach at having forgotten him, "I fear you are badly wounded!"

24

"You would think little of it, had you seen more stricken fields, young Knight," said Gaston, attempting to smile; "I am only spent with loss of blood. Bring me a draught of water, and I can ride back to the tent. But look to your prisoner, Sir Eustace."

Eustace turned to see what had become of his illustrious captive, and saw him at a little distance, speaking to a Knight on horseback. "Sir Eustace," said Bertrand, stepping towards him, "here is Sir William Beauchamp, sent by the Prince to inquire for your gallant brother, and to summon me to his tent. I leave you the more willingly that I think you have no mind for guests this evening. Farewell. I hope to be better acquainted."

Eustace had little heart to answer, but he took up Du Guesclin's sword, as if to return it to him. "Keep it, Sir Knight," said Bertrand, "you know how to wield it. I am in some sort your godfather in chivalry, and I owe you a gift. Let me have yours, that my side may not be without its wonted companion. Farewell."

"And, Sir Eustace Lynwood," said Sir William Beauchamp, riding up, "you will advance to Navaretta, where we take up our quarters in the French camp. I grieve for the loss which has befallen us this day; but I trust our chivalry has gained an equally worthy member."

Eustace bowed and, whilst Messire Bertrand mounted a horse that had been brought for his use, turned back to his own melancholy duties. The body of Sir Reginald was raised from the ground, and placed on the levelled lances of four of his men, and Eustace then assisted Gaston to rise. He tottered, leant heavily against the young Knight, and was obliged to submit to be lifted to the saddle; but neither pain, grief, nor faintness could check his flow of talk.

"Well, Eustace,—Sir Eustace, I would say,—you have seen somewhat of the chances of war."

"The mischances you mean, Gaston."

"I tell you, many a man in this host would have given his whole kindred for such luck as has befallen you. To cross swords with Du Guesclin is honour enough. This cut will be a matter of boasting to my dying day; but, to take him prisoner —"

"Nay, that was no merit of mine. Had not the rest come up, my wars had soon been over, and I had been spared this grief."

"I know what most youths would have done in your place, and been esteemed never the worse. Dropped the pennon at that first round blow that brought you to your knee, and called for quarter. Poor pennon, I deemed it gone, and would have come to your aid, but before I could recover my feet, the fight was over, and I am glad the glory is wholly yours. Knighted under a banner in a stricken field! It is a chance which befalls not one man in five hundred, and you in your first battle! But he heeds me not. He thinks only of his brother! Look up, Sir Eustace, 'tis but the chance of war. Better die under sword and shield, than like a bed-ridden old woman; better die honoured and lamented, than worn out and forgotten. Still he has not a word! Yea, and I could weep too for company, for never lived better Knight, nor one whom Squire had better cause to love!"

25

CHAPTER V

A battle in the days of chivalry was far less destructive than those of modern times. The loss in both armies at Navaretta did not amount to six hundred; and on Pedro's side but four Knights had fallen, of whom Sir Reginald Lynwood was the only Englishman.

On the following day all the four were buried in solemn state, at the church of the village of Navaretta, Sir Eustace following his brother's bier, at the head of all the men-at-arms.

On returning to his tent, Eustace found Gaston sitting on his couch, directing Guy, and old Poitevin, who had the blue crossletted pennon spread on the ground before him. Eustace expressed his wonder. "What," exclaimed Gaston, "would I see my Knight Banneret, the youngest Knight in the army, with paltry pennon! A banneret are you, dubbed in the open field, entitled to take precedence of all Knight Bachelors. Here, Leonard, bring that pennon to me, that I may see if it can be cut square."

"Poor Eleanor's pennon!" said Eustace, sadly.

"Nay, what greater honour can it have than in becoming a banner? I only grieve that this bloodstain, the noblest mark a banner can bear, is upon the swallow-tail. But what do I see? You, a belted Knight, in your plain Esquire's helmet, and the blood-stained surcoat! Ay, and not even the gilded spurs!" he exclaimed indignantly. "Would that I had seen you depart! But it was Leonard's fault. Why, man, knew you not your duty?"

"I am no Squire of Eustace Lynwood," said Ashton.

"Every Squire is bound to serve the Knight in whose company he finds himself," said d'Aubricour. "Know you not thus much of the laws of chivalry? Come, bestir yourself, that he may be better provided in future. You must present yourself to the Prince to-morrow, Sir Eustace."

"One of his Squires bade me to his presence," said the young Knight, "but I must now write these heavy tidings to my poor sister, and I am going to Father Waleran's tent to seek parchment and ink."

"And how send you the letter?"

"By the bearer of the Prince's letters to the King. Sir Richard Ferrars knows him, and will give them into his charge. So farewell, Gaston, keep quiet, and weary not yourself with my equipment."

With these words he left the tent, and Gaston, shaking his head, and throwing himself back on his deer-skins, exclaimed, "Tender and true, brave and loving! I know not what to make of Eustace Lynwood. His spirit is high as a Paladin's of old, of that I never doubted, yet is his hand as deft at writing as a clerk's, and his heart as soft as a woman's. How he sighed and wept the livelong night, when he thought none could hear him! Well, Sir Reginald was a noble Knight, and is worthily mourned, but where is the youth who would not have been more uplifted at his own honours, than downcast at his loss; and what new-made Knight ever neglected his accoutrements to write sad tidings to his sister-in-law? But," he continued, rising again, "Guy, bring me here the gilded spurs you will

26

find yonder. The best were, I know, buried with Sir Reginald, and methought there was something amiss with one rowel of the other. So it is. Speed to Maitre Ferry, the armourer, and bid him come promptly."

"And lie you still on your couch meanwhile, Master d'Aubricour," said Guy, "or there will soon be another Squire missing among the Lances of Lynwood."

"I marvel at you, d'Aubricour," said Leonard, looking up from a pasty, which he was devouring with double relish, to make up for past privations, "I marvel that you should thus weary yourself, with your fresh wound, and all for nought."

"Call you our brave young banneret nought? Shame on thee! All England should be proud of him, much more his friend and companion."

"I wish Eustace Lynwood well with all my heart," said Leonard, "but I see not why he is to be honoured above all others. Yourself, Gaston, so much older, so perfect in all exercises, you who fought with this Frenchman too, of whom they make so much, the Prince might as well have knighted you, as Eustace, who would have been down in another moment had not I made in to the rescue. Methinks if I had been the Prince, I would have inquired upon whom knighthood would sit the best."

"And the choice would have been the same," said Gaston. "Not only was Sir Eustace the captor of Messire Bertrand, whereas my luck was quite otherwise; but what would knighthood have availed the wandering landless foreigner, as you courteously term me, save to fit me for the leadership of a band of *routiers*, and unfit me for the office of an Esquire, which I do, as you say, understand indifferently well."

"Is it not the same with him?" cried Leonard. "He does not own a palm's breadth of land, and for gold, all he will ever possess is on those broken spurs of his brother's."

"Listen to me, Leonard," said Gaston. "Rich or poor, Sir Eustace is the only fit leader of the Lances till the little boy is of age, but this he could not be without knightly rank. Even in this campaign, when I might have taken the command, I being disabled for the present, it must have devolved on him, who might not have been so readily obeyed."

"No, indeed," said Leonard. "Strange that the touch of the Prince's sword should make so great a difference between him and me."

"If it was the touch of the Prince's sword that did so," said Gaston.

"What else?" sharply retorted Leonard. "Not height nor strength! His hand and arm might belong to a girl, I could crush it in my grasp." So saying, he extended a huge, hard, red palm.

"Ay?" said Gaston; "I should like to see whether that great paw would have won Du Guesclin's sword."

"I tell you flatly," proceeded Ashton, "I might follow Sir Reginald, since he was a man of substance, honoured in our country, and my father meant to oblige and do him grace by placing me with him."

"Grace!" repeated Gaston.

"But," continued Ashton, angrily, "as to serving Eustace, the clerk, no older than myself, half a head shorter, and a mere landless upstart, that my father's son

27

shall never do!"

"Say you so?" said Gaston. "I recommend you not to do so quite so loud, or perchance the landless upstart might hand your father's son over to the Provost Marshal, for preaching disaffection to his men. And, in good time, here comes the Master Armourer."

The rest of the day was spent by Gaston in the arrangement of the equipments, so important in his estimation, and scarcely another word was spoken save on the choice of helm and shield, and the adaptation of crests and blazonry. The next point for consideration was the disposal of the prisoners taken by the Lances of Lynwood in the early part of the battle. Two were Squires, the other four, rough-looking men-at-arms who protested that they could not pay one denier towards their ransom. Eustace liberated them, and was greatly inclined to do the same by the Squires; but Gaston assured him it would be doing wrong to the Prince's cause to set the rogues free without taking some good French crowns from them, and therefore, permitting him to name what ransom he thought fit, he returned to them their horses, and dismissed them to collect the sum.

Early the next morning, Gaston had the satisfaction of beholding his young banneret arrayed in knightly guise, the golden spurs on his heels, Du Guesclin's sword by his side, and his white mantle flung over his shoulder. Leonard was summoned to accompany him, but he growled out something so like an absolute refusal and utter disclaimer of all duty to Sir Eustace, that Gaston began to reproach him vehemently.

"Never mind, Gaston," said Eustace, "you never mend matters with him in that way, I shall do very well alone."

"So you shall never go," said Gaston, rising; "I will go myself, I have been longing to see you received by the Prince. Where is my sword?"

"Nay, Gaston," said Eustace, "that must not be. See how the hot sunbeams lie across that hill between us and the Prince's tent. You must not waste your strength if it is true that we are to journey to Burgos to-day."

"It shows how new your chivalry is, that you make so much of a mere scratch," said Gaston, hastily commencing his preparations; "Guy, go you and saddle Brigliador."

"No, do not touch Brigliador," said Eustace. "You deny it in vain, Gaston; your face betrays that you do not move without pain. I learnt some leech-craft among my clerkly accomplishments, and you had better take care that you do not have the benefit. Leonard, since it is the only way to quiet him, I order you to mount."

Leonard hung his head, and obeyed. They rode towards the village of Najara, where Eustace found the Prince entering the church, to hear morning mass. Giving his horse to John Ingram, he followed among the other Knights who thronged the little building.

The service at an end, he received more than one kind greeting from his brother's friends, and one of them, Sir Richard Ferrars, a fine old man, whose iron-gray locks contrasted with his ruddy complexion, led him forward to present him to the Prince of Wales.

"Welcome! our new-made Knight," said Edward. "Brave comrades, I present to

28

you the youngest brother of our order, trusting you will not envy him for having borne off the fairest rose of our chaplet of Navaretta."

Bertrand du Guesclin, who stood among the throng of nobles around the Prince, was the first to come forward and shake Eustace by the hand, saying with a laugh, "Nay, my Lord, this is the first time the ugliest Knight in France has been called by such a name. However, young Sir, may you win and wear many another."

"That scarcely may be a sincere wish, Messire Bertrand," said the Duke of Lancaster, "unless you mean roses of love instead of roses of war. And truly, with his face, and the fame he owes to you, methinks he will not find our damsels at Bordeaux very hard of heart. See, he blushes, as if we had guessed his very thought."

"Truly, my Lord John," said old Sir John Chandos sternly, "a man may well blush to hear a son of King Edward talk as if such trifling were the reward of knighthood. His face and his fame forsooth! as if he were not already in sufficient danger of being cockered up, like some other striplings on whom it has pleased his Highness to confer knighthood for as mere a chance as this."

"You have coloured his cheek in good earnest," said the Captal de Buch. "Consider, Chandos, this is no time to damp his spirit."

"It were a spirit scarce worth fostering, if it is to be damped by a little breath of the lips one way or the other," said Sir John, moving off, and adding, when out of Eustace's hearing, "A likely lad enough had he been under his brother's training, but they will spoil him, and I will have no hand in it."

Eustace had been accustomed to hold the warrior in such veneration, that he felt considerably hurt and mortified at the want of welcome which contrasted with the kindness of the rest; and he could hardly recover his self-possession sufficiently to inquire the pleasure of the Prince with regard to his brother's troop.

"Take command yourself," said Edward. "You surely have some Esquire or man-at-arms who can supply your own want of experience."

"My brother's Squire, Gaston d'Aubricour, is well learned in chivalry, my Lord," said Eustace, "and I will do my best, with his aid, to fulfil my trust."

"It is well," said Edward. "The Lances of Lynwood are too well trained easily to forget their duty, and I fear not but that you will do well. How old is your brother's young heir?"

"Eight years, my Lord."

"We will soon have him at Bordeaux," said Edward, "that he may grow up with my boys in the same friendship as their fathers. And now," added he, turning from Eustace to the assembled nobles around him, "let us part, and prepare for our further journey. In an hour's time the bugles shall summon you to depart for Burgos."

The Prince walked away towards his tent with the Captal de Buch, and Eustace looked round for his horse, which he saw at no great distance with Ingram, but Leonard Ashton was nowhere in sight. Eustace mounted, and rode towards his own tent, desiring the yeoman to seek Ashton out, while he himself proceeded slowly, musing, with feelings of considerable disappointment and vexation, on the

29

reception he had met from Sir John Chandos, the man in the whole camp whose good opinion he would have most valued. "This is folly," thought he, however, rousing himself after a minute or two of such meditations. "What said the good old Baron but what I know full well myself, that I am far from meriting my new honours? On whom does it depend, but myself to win his praise? And by our Lady's grace, I will make him confess at last, that, young as I am, I can show that I deserve my spurs. What, ho! Ingram, where is Master Ashton?"

"Where you will little like to hear of him, Sir Knight," said the yeoman, galloping up on his tall Flemish horse. "At the wine-shop, yonder, in the village, with that ill-favoured, one-eyed Squire that you wot of. I called him as you desired, and all that I got for an answer was, that he would come at his own time, and not at your bidding."

"Said he so? the ungracious, headstrong fellow!" said Eustace, looking back wistfully. "And what to do! To ride back myself might be the means of getting the whole troop late in starting, and disorderly—yet, to leave him!" Eustace looked at John Ingram's comely and stolid face, and then almost smiled at himself for seeking counsel from him. "Ride you on, John," said he; "tell Master d'Aubricour of the order to depart—let all be in readiness by the time I return."

Then turning his horse quickly, Eustace rode back to the village. All was haste and confusion there—horses were being led forth and saddled, pages, grooms, and men-at-arms hurrying to and fro—bugles sounding—everything in the bustle incident to immediate departure. He could only make his way through the press slowly, and with difficulty, which ill suited with his impatience and perplexity. In front of the venta, a low white cottage, with a wooden balcony overspread with vines, there was a still closer press, and loud vehement voices, as of disputants, were heard, while the various men-at-arms crowded in so closely to see the fray, if such it were, as to be almost regardless of the horse, which Eustace was pressing forward upon them. He looked over their heads to see Leonard, but in vain. He thought of retreat, but found himself completely entangled in the throng. At that moment, a cry was heard, "The Provost Marshal!" The crowd suddenly, he knew not how, seemed to melt away from around him, in different directions, and he found himself left, on horseback, in the midst of the little village green, amongst scattered groups of disreputable-looking yeomen, archers, and grooms, who were making what speed they could to depart, as from the other side the Provost, the archers of the guard, and Sir John Chandos entered upon the scene.

"Ha! What is all this? Whom have we here?" exclaimed the old Baron. "Sir Eustace Lynwood! By my life, a fair commencement for your dainty young knighthood!"

"On my word, my Lord Chandos," said Eustace, colouring deeply, "I am no loiterer here; I came but to seek my Squire, Leonard Ashton, and found myself entangled in the crowd."

"Ay, ay! I understand," said Chandos, without listening to him; "I see how it will be. Off to your troop instantly, Master Knight. I suppose they are all seeking Squires in the wine-shops!"

"You do me wrong, my Lord," said Eustace; "but you shall be obeyed."

30

The bugles had already sounded before he reached his own quarters, where he found that, thanks to Gaston, all was right. The tent had been taken down and packed on the baggage mules, the men were mounted, and drawn up in full array, with his banner floating above their heads; and Gaston himself was only waiting his appearance to mount a stout mule, which Martin, the horse-boy, was leading up and down.

"This is well. Thanks, good Gaston," said Eustace, with a sigh of relief, as he took off his heavy helmet, which had become much heated during his hasty ride in the hot sun.

"No news of the truant?" asked Gaston. "Who but you would have thought of going after him? Well did I know you would never prosper without me at your elbow."

Eustace smiled, but he was too much heated and vexed to give a very cheerful assent. He had only time to load Ferragus with his armour, and mount a small pony, before the signal for the march was given, and all set forth. Early in the year as it was, the sun already possessed great force, and the dry rocky soil of Castile reflected his beams, so that, long before noon, it seemed to Eustace almost as if their march lay through an oven. Nor were his perplexities by any means at an end; the thirst, occasioned by the heat, was excessive, and at every venta, in the villages through which they passed, the men called loudly for liquor; but the hot, fiery Spanish wine was, as Eustace had already been cautioned by Father Waleran, only fit to increase the evil, by inflaming their blood. It was the Holy Week, which was to him a sufficient reason for refraining entirely, contenting himself with a drink of water, when it could be procured, which, however, was but rarely. He would willingly have persuaded his men to do the same, but remonstrance was almost without effect, and his dry lips refused to utter a prohibition, which would have been esteemed at once cruel and unreasonable. In his persuasions to Gaston he was, however, more in earnest, representing to him that he was increasing the fever of his wound; but the Squire was perfectly impracticable. At first, he answered in his usual gay, careless manner, that the scratch was nothing, and that, be what it might, he had as soon die of a wound as of thirst; but as the day wore on, it seemed as if the whole nature of the man were becoming changed. Sometimes he was boisterously loud in his merriment, sometimes sullen and silent; and when Eustace, unwearied, reiterated his arguments, he replied to him, not only with complete want of the deference he was usually so scrupulous in paying to his dignity, but with rude and scurril taunts and jests on his youth, his clerkly education, and his inexperience. Eustace's patience would scarcely have held out, but that he perceived that d'Aubricour was by no means master of himself, and he saw in his flushed brow, and blood-shot eye, reason to fear for the future effect of the present excess. There was suppressed laughter among the men at some of his sallies. Without being positively in disorder, the troop did not display the well-arrayed aspect which had always hitherto distinguished the Lances of Lynwood; and poor Eustace, wearied and worn out, his right-hand man failing him, dispirited by Chandos's reproach, and feeling all the cares of the world on his shoulders, had serious thoughts of going to the Prince, and resigning the

31

command for which he was unfit.

At last he beheld the Cathedral of Burgos rising in the midst of the Moorish fortifications of the town, and, halting his men under the shade of a few trees, he rode on in search of the marshals of the camp, and as soon as the open space for his tents had been assigned, he returned to see them raised. Gaston, who had of late become more silent, was lifted from his mule, and assisted into the tent, where he was laid on his couch, and soon after, Eustace was relieved from his anxiety on Leonard Ashton's account, by his appearance. He came stumbling in without one word of apology, only declaring himself as weary as a dog, and, throwing himself down on a deer-skin on his own side of the tent, was fast asleep in another minute.

CHAPTER VI

Leonard Ashton was awakened the next morning by the light of the rising sun streaming in where the curtain of the tent had been raised to admit the fresh dewy morning air. The sunbeams fell on the hair and face of Eustace as he leant over Gaston, who lay stretched on the couch, and faintly spoke: "I tell you it is more. Such fever as this would not be caused by this trifling cut. There is sickness abroad in the camp, and why should it not be my turn as well as another man's. Take care of yourself, Sir Eustace."

No sooner did Leonard understand the sense of these words, than he sprang up, rushed out of the tent, and never rested till he thought himself at a safe distance, when he shouted to Eustace to come to him.

"Has he got this fever on him?" exclaimed he, as Eustace approached.

"He is very ill at ease," replied Eustace, "but to my mind it is caused by yesterday's fatigue and heat, added to the wine which he would drink."

"It is the fever, I say," replied Ashton; "I am sure it is. Come away, Eustace, or we shall all be infected."

"I cannot leave him," said Eustace.

"What? You do not mean to peril yourself by going near him?" said Ashton.

"I think not that there is peril in so doing," answered Eustace; "and even if there were, I could not leave him in sickness, after all his kindness to me and patience with my inexperience."

"He is no brother nor cousin to us," said Leonard. "I see not why we should endanger our lives for a stranger. I will not, for my own part; and, as your old friend and comrade, I would entreat you not."

These were kinder words than Eustace had heard from Ashton since the beginning of his jealousy, and he answered, as he thought they were meant, in a friendly tone, "Thanks, Leonard, but I cannot look on Gaston d'Aubricour as a stranger; and had I fewer causes for attachment to him, I could not leave my post."

"Only you do not expect me to do the same," said Leonard; "my father sent me here to gain honour and wealth, not to be poisoned with the breath of a man in a fever."

"Assuredly not," said Eustace. "I will arrange matters so that you shall no longer sleep in our tent. But let me ask of you, Leonard, what was the meaning of your conduct of yesterday?"

"You may ask yourself," said Leonard, sullenly; "it is plain enough, methinks."

"Have a care, Leonard. Remember that my brother's authority is given to me."

"Much good may it do you," said Leonard; "but that is nothing to me. I am no vassal of yours, to come at your call. I have my own friends, and am not going to stay in this infected part of the camp with men who keep a fever among them. Give me but my sword and mantle from the tent, and I will trouble you no more."

"Wait, Leonard, I will take all measures for your safety; but remember that I am answerable to the Prince for my brother's followers."

"Answer for your own serfs," retorted Leonard, who had nearly succeeded in working himself into a passion. "My father might be willing to grace Sir Reginald by letting me follow him, but by his death I am my own man, and not to move at your beck and call, because the Prince laid his sword on your shoulder. Knave Jasper," he called to one of the men-at-arms, "bring my sword and cloak from the tent; I enter it no more."

"I know not how far you may be bound to me," said Eustace, "and must inquire from some elder Knight, but I fear that your breaking from me may be attended with evil effects to your name and fame."

Leonard had put on his dogged expression, and would not listen. He had already set his mind on joining *le Borgne Basque*, and leaving the service which his own envious service rendered galling; and the panic excited in his mind by Gaston's illness determined him to depart without loss of time, or listening to the representations which he could not answer. He turned his back on Eustace, and busied himself with the fastenings of his sword, which had by this time been brought to him. Even yet Eustace was not rebuffed. "One more hint, Leonard. From what I am told, there is more peril to thy health in revelry than in the neighbourhood of poor Gaston. If you will quit one who wishes you well, take heed to your ways."

Still the discourteous Squire made no reply, and walked off in all the dignity of ill-humour. The young Knight, who really had a warm feeling of affection for him, stood looking after him with a sigh, and then returned to his patient, whom he found in an uneasy sleep. After a few moments' consideration, he summoned old Guy to take the part of nurse, and walked to the tent of Sir Richard Ferrars, to ask his counsel.

The old Knight, who was standing at the door of his tent, examining into some hurt which his steed had received the day before, kindly and cordially greeted Eustace on his approach. "I am glad you are not above taking advice," he said, "as many a youth might be after such fresh honours."

"I feel but too glad to find some one who will bestow advice on me," said Eustace; and he proceeded to explain his difficulties with regard to Leonard Ashton.

"Let him go! and a good riddance," said Sir Richard; "half your cares go with him."

33

"Yet I am unwilling not to attempt to hinder my old comrade from running to ruin."

"You have quite enough on your own hands already," said the old Knight; "he would do far more harm in your troop than out of it, and try your patience every hour."

"He is my old playfellow," said Eustace, still dissatisfied.

"More shame for him," said Sir Richard; "waste not another thought on so cross-grained a slip, who, as I have already feared, might prove a stumbling-block to you, so young in command as you are. Let him get sick of his chosen associates, and no better hap can befall him. And for yourself, what shall you do with this sick Squire?"

"What can I do, save to give the best attendance I may?"

"Nay, I am not the man to gainsay it. 'Tis no more than you ought. And yet—" He surveyed the young Knight's slender form and slightly moulded limbs, his cheeks pale with watching and the oppressive heat of the night, and the heavy appearance of the eyelids that shaded his dark blue thoughtful eyes. "Is your health good, young man?"

"As good as that of other men," said Eustace.

"Men!" said Sir Richard; "boys, you mean! But be a man, since you will, only take as good care of yourself as consists with duty. I had rather have you safe than a dozen of these black-visaged Gascons."

Eustace further waited to mention to Sir Richard his untoward encounter with Sir John Chandos, and to beg him to explain it to the old Baron.

"I will," said Sir Richard; "and don't take old Chandos's uncourtliness too much to heart, young Eustace. He means you no ill. Do your duty, and he will own it in time."

Eustace thanked the old Knight, and with spirits somewhat cheered, returned to his tent, there to devote himself to the service of his sick Squire. The report that the fever was in his tent made most persons willing to avoid him, and he met little interruption in his cares. Of Leonard, all that he heard was from a man-at-arms, who made his appearance in his tent to demand Master Ashton's arms, horse, and other property, he having entered the service of Sir William Felton; and Eustace was too much engaged with his own cares to make further inquiry after him.

For a day or two Gaston d'Aubricour's fever ran very high, and just when its violence was beginning to diminish, a fresh access was occasioned by the journey from Burgos to Valladolid, whither he was carried in a litter, when the army, by Pedro's desire, marched thither to await his promised subsidy. The unwholesome climate was of most pernicious effect to the whole of the English army, and in especial to the Black Prince, who there laid the foundation of the disorder which destroyed his health. Week after week passed on, each adding heat to the summer, and increasing the long roll of sick and dying in the camp, while Gaston still lay, languid and feeble by day, and fevered by night; there were other patients among the men-at-arms, requiring scarcely less care; and the young Knight himself, though, owing to his temperate habits, he had escaped the prevailing sickness, was looking thin and careworn with the numerous troubles and anxieties that were pressing on him.

Still he had actually lost not one of his men, and after the first week or two, began to have more confidence in himself, and to feel his place as their commander more than he would have done had Gaston been able to assist him. At last his trusty Squire began slowly to recover, though nightly returns of fever still kept him very weak.

"The Pyrenean breezes would make me another man," said he, one evening, when Eustace had helped him to the front of the tent, where he might enjoy the coolness which began to succeed the sultry heat of the day.

"I hear," said Eustace, "that we are to return as soon as the Prince can be moved. He is weary of waiting till this dog of a Spaniard will perform his contract."

"By my faith," said d'Aubricour, "I believe the butcherly rogue means to cancel his debts by the death of all his creditors. I would give my share of the pay, were it twenty times more, for one gust of the mountain air of my own hills."

"Which way lies your home, Gaston?" asked Eustace. "Near the pass by which we crossed?"

"No; more to the west. My home, call you it? You would marvel to see what it is now. A shattered, fire-scathed keep; the wolf's den in earnest, it may be. It is all that is left of the Castle d'Albricorte."

"How?" exclaimed Eustace. "What brought this desolation?"

"Heard you never my story?" said Gaston. "Mayhap not. You are fresh in the camp, and it is no recent news, nor do men question much whence their comrades come. Well, Albricorte was always a noted house for courage, and my father, Baron Beranger, not a whit behind his ancestors. He called himself a liegeman of England, because England was farthest off, and least likely to give him any trouble, and made war with all his neighbours in his own fashion. Rare was the prey that the old Black Wolf of the Pyrenees was wont to bring up to his lair, and right merry were the feastings there. Well I do remember how my father and brothers used to sound their horns as a token that they did not come empty-handed, and then, panting up the steep path, would come a rich merchant, whose ransom filled our purses half a year after, or a Knight, whose glittering armour made him a double prize, or—"

"What! you were actually—"

"Freebooters, after the fashion of our own Quatre fils Aymon," answered Gaston, composedly. "Yes, Beranger d'Albricorte was the terror of all around, and little was the chance that aught would pursue him to his den. So there I grew up, as well beseemed the cub of such a wolf, racing through the old halls at my will."

"Your mother?" asked Eustace.

"Ah! poor lady! I remember her not. She died when I was a babe, and all I know of her was from an old hag, the only woman in the Castle, to whom the charge of me was left. My mother was a noble Navarrese damsel whom my father saw at a tourney, seized, and bore away as she was returning from the festival. Poor lady! our grim Castle must have been a sad exchange from her green valleys—and the more, that they say she was soon to have wedded the Lord of Montagudo, the

35

victor of that tourney. The Montagudos had us in bitter feud ever after, and my father always looked like a thunderstorm if their name was spoken. They say she used to wander on the old battlements like a ghost, ever growing thinner and whiter, and scarce seemed to joy even in her babes, but would only weep over them. That angered the Black Wolf, and there were chidings which made matters little better, till at last the poor lady pined away, and died while I was still an infant."

"A sad tale," said Eustace.

"Ay! I used to weep at it, when the old crone who nursed me would tell it over as I sat by her side in the evening. See, here is holy relic that my mother wore round her neck, and my nurse hung round mine. It has never been parted from me. So I grew up to the years of pagehood, which came early with me, and forth I went on my first foray with the rest of them. But as we rode joyously home with our prey before us, a band of full a hundred and fifty men-at-arms set on us in the forest. Our brave thirty—down they went on all side. I remember the tumult, the heavy mace uplifted, and my father's shield thrust over me. I can well-nigh hear his voice saying, 'Flinch not, Gaston, my brave wolf-cub!' But then came a fall, man and horse together, and I went down stunned, and knew no more till a voice over me said, 'That whelp is stirring—another sword-thrust!' But another replied, 'He bears the features of Alienor, I cannot slay him.'"

"It was your mother's lover?"

"Montagudo? Even so; and I was about to beg for mercy, but, at my first movement, the other fellow's sword struck me back senseless once more, and when I recovered my wits, all was still, and the moonlight showed me where I was. And a fair scene to waken to! A score of dark shapes hung on the trees—our trusty men-at-arms—and my own head was resting on my dead father's breast. Us they had spared from hanging—our gentle blood did us that service; but my father and my three brethren all were stone dead. The Count de Bearn had sworn to put an end to the ravages of the Black Wolf, and, joining with the Montagudos, had done the work, like traitor villains as they were."

"And yourself, Gaston?"

"I was not so badly wounded but that I could soon rise to my feet—but where should I go? I turned towards the Castle, but the Bearnese had been there before me, and I saw flames bursting from every window. I was weak and wounded, and sank down, bleeding and bewailing, till my senses left me; and I should have died, but for two Benedictines journeying for the service of their Convent. The good brethren were in fear for their bags in going through the Black Wolf's country, but they had pity on me; they brought me to myself, and when they had heard my tale, they turned aside to give Christian burial to my father and brothers. They were holy men, those monks, and, for their sakes, I have spared the cowl ever since. They tended me nearly as well as you have done, and brought me to their Convent, where they would fain have made a monk of me, but the wolf was too strong in me, and, ere a month was passed, I had been so refractory a pupil, that they were right glad to open the Convent gates. I walked forth to seek my fortune, without a denier, with nothing but the sword I had taken from my father's hand,

and borne with me, much against the good men's will. I meant to seek service with any one who would avenge me on the Count de Bearn. One night I slept on the hill-side, one day I fasted, the next I fell in with Sir Perduccas d'Albret's troop. I had seen him in my father's company. He heard my tale, saw me a strong, spirited lad, and knew a d'Aubricour would be no discredit to his free lances. So he took me as his page, and thence—but the tale would be long—I became what you see me."

"And you have never seen your own Castle again?"

"But once. D'Albret laughed when I called on him to revenge me on the Count de Bearn, and bade me bide my time till I met him in battle. As to my heritage, there was no hope for that. Once, when I had just broken with Sir Nele Loring, and left his troop, and times were hard with me, I took my horse and rode to Albricorte, but there was nought but the bare mountain, and the walls black with fire. There was, indeed, a wretched shepherd and his wife, who trembled and looked dismayed when they found that one of the Albricortes still lived; but I could get nothing from them, unless I had taken a sheep before me on the saddle; so I rode off again to seek some fresh service, and, by good hap, lit on Sir Reginald just as old Harwood was dead. All I have from my father is my name, my shield, and an arm that I trust has disgraced neither."

"No, indeed. Yours is a strange history, Gaston; such as we dream not of in our peaceful land. Homeless, friendless, I know not how you can be thus gay spirited?"

"A light heart finds its way through the world the easiest," said Gaston, smiling. "I have nothing to lose, and no sorrows to waste time on. But are you not going forth this cool evening, Sir Eustace? you spoke of seeking fresh tidings of the Prince."

Eustace accordingly walked forth, attended by his yeoman, John Ingram; but all he could learn was, that Edward had sent a remonstrance to the King of Castile on the delay of the subsidy.

CHAPTER VII

As Eustace was returning, his attention was caught by repeated groans, which proceeded from a wretched little hovel almost level with the earth. "Hark!" said he to Ingram, a tall stout man-at-arms from the Lynwood estate. "Didst thou not hear a groaning?"

"Some of the Castilians, Sir. To think that the brutes should be content to live in holes not fit for swine!"

"But methought it was an English tongue. Listen, John!"

And in truth English ejaculations mingled with the moans: "To St. Joseph of Glastonbury, a shrine of silver! Blessed Lady of Taunton, a silver candlestick! Oh! St. Dunstan!"

Eustace doubted no longer; and stooping down and entering the hut, he beheld, as well as the darkness would allow him, Leonard Ashton himself, stretched on some mouldy rushes, and so much altered, that he could scarcely have been recognized as the sturdy, ruddy youth who had quitted the Lances of Lynwood but five weeks before.

"Eustace! Eustace!" he exclaimed, as the face of his late companion appeared. "Can it be you? Have the saints sent you to my succour?"

"It is I, myself, Leonard," replied Eustace; "and I hope to aid you. How is it—"

"Let me feel your hand, that I may be sure you are flesh and blood," cried Ashton, raising himself and grasping Eustace's hand between his own, which burnt like fire; then, lowering his voice to a whisper of horror, "She is a witch!"

"Who?" asked Eustace, making the sign of the cross.

Leonard pointed to a kind of partition which crossed the hut, beyond which Eustace could perceive an old hag-like woman, bending over a cauldron which was placed on the fire. Having made this effort, he sank back, hiding his face with his cloak, and trembling in every limb. A thrill of dismay passed over the Knight, and the giant, John Ingram, stood shaking like an aspen, pale as death, and crossing himself perpetually. "Oh, take me from this place, Eustace," repeated Leonard, "or I am a dead man, both body and soul!"

"But how came you here, Leonard?"

"I fell sick some three days since, and—and, fearing infection, Sir William Felton bade me be carried from his lodgings; the robbers, his men-at-arms, stripped me of all I possessed, and brought me to this dog-hole, to the care of this old hag. Oh, Eustace, I have heard her mutter prayers backwards; and last night—oh! last night! at the dead hour, there came in a procession—of that I would take my oath—seven black cats, each holding a torch with a blue flame, and danced around me, till one laid his paw upon my breast, and grew and grew, with its flaming eyes fixed on me, till it was as big as an ox, and the weight was intolerable, the while her spells were over me, and I could not open my lips to say so much as an Ave Mary. At last, the cold dew broke out on my brow, and I should have been dead in another instant, when I contrived to make the sign of the Cross, whereat they all whirled wildly round, and I fell—oh! I fell miles and miles downwards, till at last I found myself, at morning's light, with the hateful old witch casting water in my face. Oh, Eustace, take me away!"

Such were the times, that Eustace Lynwood, with all his cool sense and mental cultivation, believed implicitly poor Leonard's delirious fancy—black cats and all; and the glances he cast at the poor old Spaniard were scarcely less full of terror and abhorrence, as he promised Leonard, whom he now regarded only in the light of his old comrade, that he should, without loss of time, be conveyed to his own tent.

"But go not—leave me not," implored Leonard, clinging fast to him, almost like a child to its nurse, with a hand which was now cold as marble.

"No; I will remain," said Eustace; "and you, Ingram, hasten to bring four of the men with the litter in which Master d'Aubricour came from Burgos. Hasten I tell you."

Ingram, with his eyes dilated with horror, appeared but too anxious to quit this den, yet lingered. "I leave you not here, Sir Knight."

"Thanks, thanks, John," replied the youth; "but remain I must, and will. As a

Christian man, I defy the foul fiend and all his followers!"

John departed. Never was Leonard so inclined to rejoice in his friend's clerkly education, or in his knighthood, which was then so much regarded as a holy thing, that the presence of one whose entrance into the order was so recent was deemed a protection. The old woman, a kind-hearted creature in the main, though, certainly forbidding-looking in her poverty and ugliness, was rejoiced to see her patient visited by a friend. She came towards them, addressing Eustace with what he took for a spell, though, had he understood Spanish he would have found it a fine flowing compliment. Leonard shrank closer to him, pressed his hand faster, and he, again crossing himself, gave utterance to a charm. Spanish, especially old Castilian, had likeness enough to Latin for the poor old woman to recognize its purport; she poured out a voluble vindication, which the two young men believed to be an attempt at further bewitching them. Eustace, finding his Latin rather the worse for wear, had recourse to all the strange rhymes, or exorcisms, English, French, or Latin, with which his memory supplied him. Thanks to these, the sorceress was kept at bay, and the spirits of his terrified companion were sustained till the arrival of all the Lances of Lynwood, headed by Gaston himself, upon his mule, in the utmost anxiety for his Knight, looking as gaunt and spectral as the phantoms they dreaded. He blessed the saints when Eustace came forth safe and sound, and smiled and shook his head with an arch look when Leonard was carried out; but his never-failing good-nature prevented him from saying a word which might savour of reproach when he saw to what a condition the poor youth was reduced. As four stout men-at-arms took up the litter, the old woman, coming forth to her threshold, uttered something which his knowledge of the Romanesque tongues of Southern France enabled him to interpret into a vindication of her character, and a request for a reward for her care of the sick Englishman.

"Throw her a gold piece, Sir Eustace, or she may cast at you an evil eye. There, you old hag," he added in the Provencal patois, "take that, and thank your stars that 'tis not with a fire that your tender care, as you call it, is requited."

The men-at-arms meditated ducking the witch after their own English fashion, but it was growing late and dark, and the Knight gave strict orders that they should keep together in their progress to their own tents. Here Leonard was deposited on the couch which Gaston insisted on giving up to him; but his change of residence appeared to be of little advantage, for the camp was scarce quiet for the night, before he shrieked out that the black cats were there. Neither Eustace nor Gaston could see them, but that was only a proof that they were not under the power of the enchantment, and John Ingram was quite sure that he had not only seen the sparkle of their fiery eyes, but felt the scratch of their talons, which struck him to the ground, with his foot caught in the rope of the tent, while he was walking about with his eyes shut.

The scratch was actually on his face the next morning, and he set out at the head of half the Lances of Lynwood to find the poor old woman, and visit her with condign punishment; but she was not forthcoming, and they were obliged to content themselves with burning her house, assisted by a host of idlers. In the meantime, Sir Eustace had called in the aid of the clergy: the chaplains of the camp came in procession, sprinkled the patient's bed with holy water, and uttered an exorcism, but without availing to prevent a third visit from the enemy. After this, however, Leonard's fever began to abate, and he ceased to be haunted.

He had been very ill; and, thoroughly alarmed, he thought himself dying, and bitterly did he repent of the headstrong insubordination and jealously which had lead him to quit his best and only friend. He had not, indeed, the refinement of feeling which would have made Eustace's generosity his greatest reproach; he clung to him as his support, and received his attentions almost as a right; but still he was sensible that he had acted like a fool, and that such friendship was not to be thrown away; and when he began to recover he showed himself subdued, to a certain degree grateful, and decidedly less sullen and more amenable to authority.

In the meantime, the Prince of Wales found himself sufficiently recovered to undertake to return to Aquitaine, and, weary of the treacherous delays and flagrant crimes of his ally, he resolved to quit this fatal land of Castile.

There was a general cry of joy throughout the camp when orders were given that the tents should be struck and the army begin its march in the early coolness of the next morning; and, without further adventure, the Black Prince led his weakened and reduced forces over the Pyrenees back into France. Here they were again dispersed, as the war was at an end; and the young Sir Eustace Lynwood received high commendation from the Prince, and even from Chandos himself, for being able to show his brother's band as complete in numbers and discipline as on the day when it was given into his charge.

"This," as Chandos said, "was a service which really showed him worthy of his spurs, if he would but continue the good course."

The peace with France, however, prevented the Prince from being desirous of keeping up the Lances of Lynwood, and he therefore offered to take their young leader into his own troop of Knights, who were maintained at his own table, and formed a part of his state; and so distinguished was this body, that no higher favour could have been offered. Edward likewise paid to Sir Eustace a considerable sum as the purchase of his illustrious captive, and this, together with the ransoms of the two other prisoners, enabled him to reward the faithful men-at-arms, some of whom took service with other Knights, and others returned to England. Leonard Ashton having no pleasant reminiscences of his first campaign, and having been stripped of all his property by his chosen associates, was desirous of returning to his father; and Eustace, after restoring his equipments to something befitting an Esquire of property, and liberally supplying him with the expenses of his journey, bade him an affectionate farewell, and saw him depart, not without satisfaction at no longer feeling himself accountable for his conduct.

"There he goes," said Gaston, "and I should like to hear the tales he will amaze the good Somersetshire folk with. I trow he will make them believe that he took Du Guesclin himself, and that the Prince knighted you by mistake."

"His tale of the witches will be something monstrous," said Eustace; "but still, methinks he is much the better for his expedition: far less crabbed in temper, and less clownish in manners."

"Ay," said Gaston, "if he were never to be under any other guidance than yours, I think the tough ash-bough might be moulded into something less unshapely. You have a calmness and a temper such as he cannot withstand, nor I understand. 'Tis not want of spirit, but it is that you never seem to take or see what is meant for affront. I should think it tameness in any other."

"Well, poor fellow, I wish he may prosper," said Eustace. "But now, Gaston, to our own affairs. Let us see what remains of the gold."

"Ah! your bounty to our friend there has drawn deeply on our purse," said Gaston.

"It shall not be the worse for you, Gaston, for I had set aside these thirty golden crowns for you before I broke upon my own store. It is not such a recompense as Reginald or I myself would have wished after such loving and faithful service; but gold may never recompense truth."

"As for recompense," said Gaston, "I should be by a long score the debtor if we came to that. If it had not been for Sir Reginald, I should be by this time a reckless freebooter, without a hope in this world or the next; if it had not been for you, these bones of mine would long since have been picked by my cousins, the Spanish wolves. But let the gold tarry in your keeping: it were better King Edward's good crowns should not be, after all else that has been, in my hands."

"But, Gaston, you will need fitting out for the service of Sir William Beauchamp."

"What! What mean you, Sir Eustace?" cried Gaston. "What have I done that you should dismiss me from your followers?"

"Nay, kind Gaston, it were shame that so finished a Squire should be bound down by my poverty to be the sole follower of a banner which will never again be displayed at the head of such a band as the Lances of Lynwood."

"No, Sir Eustace, I leave you not. Recall your brother's words, 'Go not back to old ways and comrades,' quoth he; and if you cast me off, what else is left for me? for having once served a banneret, no other shall have my service. Where else should I find one who would care a feather whether I am dead or alive? So there it ends—put up your pieces, or rather, give me one wherewith to purvey a new bridle for Brigliador, for the present is far from worthy of his name."

Accordingly, the Gascon Squire still remained attached to Eustace's service, while the trusty Englishman, John Ingram, performed the more menial offices. Time sped away at the court of Bordeaux; the gallant Du Guesclin was restored to liberty, after twice paying away his ransom for the deliverance of his less renowned brethren in captivity, and Enrique of Trastamare, returning to Castile, was once more crowned by the inhabitants. His brother Pedro, attempting to assassinate him, fell by his hand, and all the consequences of the English expedition were undone—all, save the wasting disease that preyed on England's heir, and the desolation at the orphaned hearth of Lynwood Keep.

41

CHAPTER VIII

Two years had passed since the fight of Navaretta, when Sir Eustace Lynwood received, by the hands of a Knight newly arrived from England, a letter from Father Cyril, praying him to return home as soon as possible, since his sister-in-law, Dame Eleanor, was very sick, and desired to see him upon matters on which more could not be disclosed by letter.

Easily obtaining permission to leave Bordeaux, he travelled safely through France, and crossing from Brittany, at length found himself once more in Somersetshire. It was late, and fast growing dark, when he rode through Bruton; but, eager to arrive, he pushed on, though twilight had fast faded into night, and heavy clouds, laden with brief but violent showers, were drifting across the face of the moon. On they rode, in silence, save for Gaston's execrations of the English climate, and the plashing of the horses' feet in the miry tracks, along which, in many places, the water was rushing in torrents.

At length they were descending the long low hill, or rather undulation, leading to the wooded vale of Lynwood, and the bright lights of the Keep began to gleam like stars in the darkness—stars indeed to the eager eyes of the young Knight, who gazed upon them long and affectionately, as he felt himself once more at home. "I wonder," said he, "to see the light strongest towards the east end of the Castle! I knew not that the altar lights in the chapel could be seen so far!" Then riding on more quickly, and approaching more nearly, he soon lost sight of them behind the walls, and descending the last little rising ground, the lofty mass of building rose huge and black before him.

He wound his bugle and rode towards the gate, but at the moment he expected to cross the drawbridge, Ferragus suddenly backed, and he perceived that it was raised. "This is some strange chance!" said he, renewing the summons, but in vain, for the echoes of the surrounding woods were the only reply. "Ralph must indeed be deaf!" said he.

"Let him be stone deaf," said Gaston; "he is not the sole inhabitant of the Castle. Try them again, Sir Eustace."

"Hark!—methought I heard the opening of the hall door!" said Eustace. "No! What can have befallen them?"

"My teeth are chattering with cold," said Gaston, "and the horses will be ruined with standing still in the driving rain. Cannot we betake ourselves to the village hostel, and in the morning reproach them with their churlishness?"

"I must be certified that there is nothing amiss," said Sir Eustace, springing from his saddle; "I can cross the moat on one of the supports of the bridge."

"Have with you then, Sir Knight," said Gaston, also leaping to the ground, while Eustace cautiously advanced along the narrow frame of wood on which the drawbridge had rested, slippery with the wet, and rendered still more perilous by the darkness. Gaston followed, balancing himself with some difficulty, and at last they safely reached the other side. Eustace tried the heavy gates, but found them fastened on the inside with a ponderous wooden bar. "Most strange!" muttered he; "yet come on, Gaston, I can find an entrance, unless old Ralph be more on the alert than I expect."

Creeping along between the walls and the moat, till they had reached the opposite side of the Keep, Eustace stopped at a low doorway; a slight click was heard, as of a latch yielding to his hand, the door opened, and he led the way up a stone staircase in the thickness of the wall, warning his follower now and then of a broken step. After a long steep ascent, Gaston heard another door open, and though still in total darkness, perceived that they had gained a wider space. "The passage from the hall to the chapel," whispered the Knight, and feeling by the wall, they crept along, until a buzz of voices reached their ears, and light gleamed beneath a heavy dark curtain which closed the passage. Pausing for an instant, they heard a voice tremulous with fear and eagerness: "It was himself! tall plume, bright armour! the very crosslet on his breast could be seen in the moonlight! Oh! it was Sir Reginald himself, and the wild young French Squire that fell with him in Spain!"

There was a suppressed exclamation of horror, and a sound of crowding together, and at that moment, Eustace, drawing aside the curtain, advanced into the light, and was greeted by a frightful shriek, which made him at first repent of having alarmed his sister, but the next glance showed him that her place was empty, and a thrill of dismay made him stand speechless and motionless, as he perceived that the curtain he grasped was black, and the hall completely hung with the same colour.

The servants remained huddled in terror round the hearth, and the pause was first broken by a fair-faced boy, who, breaking from the trembling circle, came forward, and in a quivering tone said, "Sir, are you my father's spirit?"

Gaston's laugh came strangely on the scene, but Eustace, bending down, and holding out his hand, said, "I am your uncle Eustace, Arthur. Where is your mother?"

Arthur, with a wild cry of joy, sprung to his neck, and hid his face on his shoulder; and at the same moment old Ralph, with uplifted hands, cried, "Blessing on the Saints that my young Lord is safe, and that mine eyes have seen you once again."

"But where, oh! where is my sister?" again demanded Eustace, as his eye met that of Father Cyril, who, summoned by the screams of the servants, had just entered the hall.

"My son," replied the good Father, solemnly, "your sister is where the wicked may trouble her no more. It is three days now since she departed from this world of sorrow."

"Oh, had she but lived to see this day," said Ralph Penrose, "her cares would have been over!"

"Her prayers are answered," said Father Cyril. "Come with me, my son Eustace, if you would take a last look of her who loved and trusted you so well."

Eustace followed him to the chamber where the Lady Eleanor Lynwood lay extended on her bed. Her features were pinched and sharpened, and bore traces of her long, wasting sufferings, but they still looked lovely, though awful in their perfect calmness. Eustace knelt and recited the accustomed prayers, and then

43

stood gazing on the serene face, with a full heart, and gathering tears in his eyes, for he had loved the gentle Eleanor with the trusting affection of a younger brother. He thought of that joyous time, the first brilliant day of his lonely childhood, when the gay bridal cavalcade came sweeping down the hill, and he, half in pleasure, half in shyness, was led forth by his mother to greet the fair young bride of his brother. How had she brightened the dull old Keep, and given, as it were, a new existence to himself, a dreamy, solitary boy—how patiently and affectionately had she tended his mother, and how pleasant were the long evenings when she had unwearily listened to his beloved romances, and his visions of surpassing achievements of his own! No wonder that he wept for her as a brother would weep for an elder sister.

Father Cyril, well pleased to perceive that the kindly tenderness of his heart was still untouched by his intercourse with the world, let him gaze on for some time in silence, then laying his hand on his arm said, "She is in peace. Mourn not that her sorrows are at an end, her tears wiped away, but prepare to fulfil her last wishes, those prayers in answer to which, as I fully believe, the Saints have sent you at the very moment of greatest need."

"Her last wishes?" said Eustace. "They shall be fulfilled to the utmost as long as I have life or breath! Oh! had I but come in time to hear them from herself, and give her my own pledge."

"Grieve not that her trust was not brought down to aught of earth," said Father Cyril. "She trusted in Heaven, and died in the sure belief that her child would be guarded; and lo, his protector is come, if, as I well believe, my son Eustace, you are not changed from the boy who bade us farewell three years ago."

"If I am changed, it is not in my love for home, and for all who dwell there," said Eustace, "or rather, I love them better than before. Little did I dream what a meeting awaited me!" Again there was a long pause, which Eustace at length broke by saying, "What is the need you spoke of? What danger do you fear?"

"This is no scene for dwelling on the evil deeds of wicked men otherwise than to pray for them," said the Priest; "but return with me to the hall, and you shall hear."

Eustace lingered a few moments longer, before, heaving a deep sigh he returned to the hall, where he found Gaston and Ingram, just come in from attending to the horses, and Ralph hurrying the servants in setting out an ample meal for the travellers.

"My good old friend," said Eustace, holding out his hand as he entered, "I have not greeted you aright. You must throw the blame on the tidings that took from me all other thought, Ralph; for never was there face which I was more rejoiced to see.

"It was the blame of our own reception of you, Sir Eustace," said old Penrose. "I could tear my hair to think that you should have met with no better welcome than barred gates and owlet shrieks; but did you but know how wildly your bugle-blast rose upon our ear, while we sat over the fire well-nigh distraught with sorrow, you would not marvel that we deemed that the spirit of our good Knight might be borne upon the moaning wind."

44

"Yet," said Arthur, "I knew the note, and would have gone to the turret window, but that Mistress Cicely held me fast; and when they sent Jocelyn to look, the cowardly knave brought back the tale which you broke short."

"Boast not, Master Arthur," said Gaston; "you believed in our ghostship as fully as any of them."

"But met us manfully," said Eustace. "But why all these precautions? Why the drawbridge raised? That could scarce be against a ghost."

"Alas! Sir Eustace, there are bodily foes abroad!" said Ralph. "By your leave, Master d'Aubricour," as Gaston was about to assist his Knight in unfastening his armour, "none shall lay a hand near Sir Eustace but myself on this first night of his return; thanks be to St. Dunstan that he has come!" Eustace stood patiently for several minutes while the old man fumbled with his armour, and presently came the exclamation, "A plague on these new-fangled clasps which a man cannot undo for his life! 'Twas this low corselet that was the death of good Sir Reginald. I always said that no good would come of these fashions!"

In process of time, Eustace was disencumbered of his heavy armour; but when he stood before him in his plain dress of chamois leather, old Ralph shook his head, disappointed that he had not attained the height or the breadth of the stalwart figures of his father and brother, but was still slight and delicate looking. The golden spurs and the sword of Du Guesclin, however, rejoiced the old man's heart, and touching them almost reverentially, he placed the large arm-chair at the head of the table, and began eagerly to invite him to eat.

Eustace was too sorrowful and too anxious to be inclined for food, and long before his followers had finished their meal, he turned from the table, and asked for an account of what had befallen in his absence; for there was at that time no more idea of privacy in conversation than such as was afforded by the comparative seclusion of the party round the hearth, consisting of the Knight, his arm around his little nephew, who was leaning fondly against him; of Father Cyril, of Gaston, and old Ralph, in his wonted nook, his elbow on his knee, and his chin on his hand, feasting his eyes with the features of his beloved pupil. In answer to the query, "Who is the enemy you fear?" there was but one answer, given in different tones, "The Lord de Clarenham!"

"Ha!" cried Eustace, "it was justly then that your father, Arthur, bade me beware of him when he committed you to my charge on the battle-field of Navaretta."

"Did he so?" exclaimed Father Cyril. "Did he commit the boy to your guardianship? Formally and before witnesses?"

"I can testify to it, good Father," said Gaston. "Ay! and you, Ingram, must have been within hearing—to say nothing of Du Guesclin."

"And Leonard Ashton," said Ingram.

"It is well," said Father Cyril; "he will be here to-morrow to be confronted with Clarenham. It is the personal wardship that is of chief importance, and dwelt most on my Lady's mind."

"Clarenham lays claim then to the guardianship?" asked Eustace.

Father Cyril proceeded with a narrative, the substance of which was as follows:
—Simon de Clarenham, as has been mentioned, had obtained from King Edward,

45

in the days of the power of Isabel and Mortimer, a grant of the manor of Lynwood, but on the fall of the wicked Queen, the rightful owner had been reinstated, without, however, any formal revocation of the unjust grant. Knowing it would cost but a word of Sir Reginald to obtain its recall, both Simon and Fulk de Clarenham had done their best to make him forget its existence; but no sooner did the news of his death reach England, than Fulk began to take an ungenerous advantage of the weakness of his heir. He sent a summons for the dues paid by vassals to their Lord on a new succession, and on Eleanor's indignant refusal, followed it up by a further claim to the wardship of the person of Arthur himself, both in right of his alleged feudal superiority, and as the next of kin who was of full age. Again was his demand refused, and shortly after Lady Lynwood's alarms were brought to a height by an attempt on his part to waylay her son and carry him off by force, whilst riding in the neighbourhood of the Castle. The plot had failed, by the fidelity of the villagers of Lynwood, but the shock to the lady had increased the progress of the decay of her health, already undermined by grief. She never again trusted her son beyond the Castle walls; she trembled whenever he was out of her sight, and many an hour did she spend kneeling before the altar in the chapel. On her brother-in-law, Sir Eustace, her chief hope was fixed; on him she depended for bringing Arthur's case before the King, and, above all, for protecting him from the attacks of the enemy of his family, rendered so much more dangerous by his relationship. She did not believe that actual violence to Arthur's person was intended, but Fulk's house had of late become such an abode of misrule, that his mother and sister had been obliged to leave it for a Convent, and the tales of the lawlessness which there prevailed were such that she would have dreaded nothing more for her son than a residence there, even if Fulk had no interest in oppressing him.

That Eustace should return to take charge of his nephew before her death was her chief earthly wish, and when she found herself rapidly sinking, and the hope of its fulfilment lessening, she obtained a promise from Father Cyril that he would conduct the boy to the Abbey of Glastonbury, and there obtain from the Abbot protection for him until his uncle should return, or the machinations of Fulk be defeated by an appeal to the King.

This was accordingly Father Cyril's intention. It was unavoidable that Fulk, the near kinsman of the deceased, should be present at the funeral, but Father Cyril had intended to keep Arthur within the sanctuary of the chapel until he could depart under the care of twelve monks of Glastonbury, who were coming in the stead of the Abbot—he being, unfortunately, indisposed. Sir Philip Ashton had likewise been invited, in the hope that his presence might prove a check upon Clarenham.

CHAPTER IX

With the first dawn of morning, the chapel bell began to toll, and was replied to by the deeper sound of the bell of the parish church. Soon the court began to be filled with the neighbouring villagers, with beggars, palmers, mendicant friars of

46

all orders, pressing to the buttery-hatch, where they received the dole of bread, meat, and ale, from the hands of the pantler, under the direction of the almoner of Glastonbury, who requested their prayers for the soul of the noble Sir Reginald Lynwood, and Dame Eleanor of Clarenham, his wife. The peasantry of Lynwood, and the beggars, whose rounds brought them regularly to the Keep of Lynwood, and who had often experienced the bounty of the departed lady, replied with tears and blessings. There were not wanting the usual though incongruous accompaniments of such a scene—the jugglers and mountebanks, who were playing their tricks in one corner.

Within the hall, all was in sad, sober, and solemn array, contrasting with the motley concourse in the court. Little Arthur, dressed in black, stood by the side of his uncle, to receive the greetings of his yeoman vassals, as they came in, one by one, with clownish courtesy, but hearty respect and affection, and great satisfaction at the unexpected appearance of the young Knight.

Next came in long file, mounted on their sleek mules, the twelve monks of Glastonbury, whom the Knight and his nephew reverently received at the door, and conducted across the hall to the chapel, where the parish Priest, Father Cyril, and some of the neighbouring clergy had been chanting psalms since morning light. On the way Sir Eustace held some conference with the chief, Brother Michael, who had come prepared to assist in conveying Arthur, if possible, to Glastonbury, but was very glad to find that the Knight was able to take upon himself the charge of his nephew, without embroiling the Abbey with so formidable an enemy as Lord de Clarenham.

The next arrival was Sir Philip Ashton and his son, who could hardly believe their eyes when Eustace met them. Leonard's manner was at first cordial; but presently, apparently checked by some sudden recollection, he drew back, and stood in sheepish embarrassment, fumbling with his dagger, while Sir Philip was lavishing compliments on Eustace, who was rejoiced when the sound of horses made it necessary to go and meet Lord de Clarenham at the door. Arthur looked up in Sir Fulk's face, with a look in which curiosity and defiance were expressed; while Fulk, on his side, was ready to grind his teeth with vexation at the unexpected sight of the only man who could interfere with his projects. Then he glanced at his own numerous and well-appointed retinue, compared them with the small number of the Lynwood vassals, and with another look at his adversary's youthful and gentle appearance, he became reassured, and returned his salutations with haughty ceremony.

The whole company moved in solemn procession towards the chapel, where the mass and requiem were chanted, and the corpse of the Lady Eleanor, inclosed in a stone coffin, was lowered to its resting-place, in the vault of her husband's ancestors.

It was past noon when the banquet was spread in the hall; a higher table on the dais for the retainers and yeomanry, the latter of whom were armed with dagger, short sword, or quarter-staff.

Sir Philip Ashton and Brother Michael were chiefly at the expense of the conversation, Eustace meanwhile doing the honours with grave courtesy, taking

47

care to keep his nephew by his side. There was no one who did not feel as if on the eve of a storm; but all was grave and decorous; and at length Brother Michael and the monks of Glastonbury, rejoicing that they, at least, had escaped a turmoil, took their leave, mounted their mules, and rode off, in all correctness of civility toward the house of Lynwood, which, as Eustace could not help feeling, they thus left to fight its own battles.

"It waxes late," said Lord de Clarenham, rising; "bring out the horses, Miles; and you, my young kinsman, Arthur, you are to be my guest from henceforth. Come, therefore, prepare for the journey."

Arthur held fast by the hand of his uncle, who replied, "I thank you in my nephew's name for your intended hospitality, but I purpose at once to conduct him to Bordeaux, to be enrolled among the Prince's pages."

"Conduct him to Bordeaux, said the Knight?" answered Sir Fulk with a sneer; "to Bordeaux forsooth! It is well for you, my fair young cousin, that I have other claims to you, since, were you once out of England, I can well guess who would return to claim the lands of Lynwood."

"What claim have you to his wardship, Sir Fulk?" asked Eustace, coldly, disdaining to take notice of the latter part of this speech.

"As his feudal superior, and his nearest relation of full age," replied Clarenham.

"There are many here who can prove that it is twenty-one years past, since I was born on the feast of St. Eustace," replied the young Knight. "The house of Lynwood owns no master beneath the King of England, and the wardship of my nephew was committed to me by both his parents. Here is a witness of the truth of my words. Holy Father, the parchment!"

Father Cyril spread a thick roll, with heavy seals, purporting to be the last will and testament of Dame Eleanor Lynwood, bequeathing the wardship and marriage of her son to her beloved brother, Sir Eustace Lynwood, Knight Banneret, and, in his absence, to the Lord Abbot of Glastonbury, and Cyril Langton, Clerk.

"It is nought," said Clarenham, pushing it from him; "the Lady of Lynwood had no right to make a will in this manner, since she unlawfully detained her son from me, his sole guardian."

"The force of the will may be decided by the King's justices," said Eustace; "but my rights are not founded on it alone. My brother, Sir Reginald, with his last words, committed his son to my charge."

"What proof do you bring, Sir Eustace?" said Fulk. "I question not your word, but something more is needed in points of law, and you can scarcely expect the world to believe that Sir Reginald would commit his only child to the guardianship of one so young, and the next heir."

"I am here to prove it, my Lord," said Gaston, eagerly. "'To your care I commit him, Eustace,' said Sir Reginald, as he lay with his head on his brother's breast; and methought he also added, 'Beware of Clarenham.' Was it not so, friend Leonard?"

Leonard's reply was not readily forthcoming. His father was whispering in his ear, whilst he knit his brow, shuffled with his feet, and shrugged his shoulder disrespectfully in his father's face.

"Speak, Master Ashton," said Clarenham, in a cold incredulous tone, and bending on father and son glances which were well understood. "To your testimony, respectable and uninterested, credit must be added."

"What mean you by that, Sir Fulk de Clarenham?" cried Gaston; "for what do you take me and my word?"

"Certain tales of you and your companions, Sir Squire," answered Clarenham, "do not dispose me to take a Gascon's word for more than it is worth."

"This passes!" cried Gaston, striking his fist on the table; "you venture it because you are not of my degree! Here, ye craven Squires, will not one of you take up my glove, when I cast back in his teeth your master's foul slander of an honourable Esquire?"

"Touch it not, I command you," said Clarenham, "unless Master d'Aubricour will maintain that he never heard of a certain one-eyed Basque, and never rode on a free-booting foray with the robber Knight, Perduccas d'Albret."

"What of that?" fiercely cried Gaston.

"Quite enough, Sir Squire," said Fulk, coolly.

Gaston was about to break into a tempest of rage, when Eustace's calm voice and gesture checked him.

"Sir Fulk," said Eustace, "were you at Bordeaux, you would know that no man's word can be esteemed more sacred, or his character more high, than that of Gaston d'Aubricour."

"But in the meantime," said Clarenham, "we must be content to take that, as well as much besides, on your own assertion, Sir Eustace. Once more, Master Leonard Ashton, let me hear your testimony, as to the dying words of Sir Reginald Lynwood. I am content to abide by them."

"Come, Leonard," said his father, who had been whispering with him all this time, "speak up; you may be grieved to disappoint a once-friendly companion, but you could not help the defect of your ears."

"Sir Philip, I pray you not to prompt your son," said Eustace. "Stand forth, Leonard, on your honour. Did you or did you not hear the words of my brother, as he lay on the bank of the Zadorra?"

Leonard half rose, as if to come towards him, but his father held him fast; he looked down, and muttered, "Ay, truly, I heard Sir Reginald say somewhat."

"Tell it out, then."

"He thanked the Prince for knighting you—he prayed him to have charge of his wife and child—he bade Gaston not to return to evil courses," said Leonard, bringing out his sentences at intervals.

"And afterwards," said Eustace sternly—"when the Prince was gone? On your honour, Leonard."

Leonard almost writhed himself beneath the eyes that Eustace kept steadily fixed on him. "Somewhat—somewhat he might have said of knightly training for his son—but—but what do I know?" he added, as his father pressed hard on his foot; "it was all in your ear, for as he lay on your breast, his voice grew so faint, that I could hear little through my helmet."

49

"Nay, Master Ashton," said John Ingram, pressing forward, "if I remember right, you had thrown off your helmet, saying it was as hot as a copper cauldron; and besides, our good Knight, when he said those words touching Master Arthur, raised himself up somewhat, and spoke out louder, as if that we might all hear and bear witness."

"No witness beyond your own train, Sir Eustace?" said Clarenham.

"None," said Eustace, "excepting one whose word even you will scarcely dare to dispute, Sir Bertrand du Guesclin."

"I dispute no man's word, Sir Eustace," said Fulk; "I only say that until the claim which you allege be proved in the King's Court, I am the lawful guardian of the lands and person of the heir of Lynwood. The Lord Chancellor Wykeham may weigh the credit to be attached to the witness of this highly respectable Esquire, or this long-eared man-at-arms, or may send beyond seas for the testimony of Du Guesclin: in the meantime, I assume my office. Come here, boy."

"I will not come to you, Lord Fulk," said Arthur; "or when I do, it shall be sword in hand to ask for an account for the tears you have made my sweet mother shed."

"Bred up in the same folly!" said Fulk. "Once more, Sir Eustace, will you yield him to me, or must I use force?"

"I have vowed before his mother's corpse to shield him from you," returned Eustace.

"Think of the consequences, Sir Eustace," said Sir Philip Ashton, coming up to him. "Remember the unrepealed grant to the Clarenhams. The Lynwood manor may be at any moment resumed, to which, failing your nephew, you are heir. You will ruin him and yourself."

"It is his person, not his lands, that I am bound to guard," said Eustace. "Let him do his worst; my nephew had better be a landless man, than one such as Fulk would make him."

"Think," continued Sir Philip, "of the disadvantages to your cause of provoking a fray at such a time. Hold your hand, and yield the boy, at least till the cause come before the Chancellor."

"Never," said Eustace. "His parents have trusted him to me, and I will fulfil my promise. The scandal of the fray be on him who occasions it."

"Recollect, my Lord," said Ashton, turning to Fulk, "that this may be misrepresented. These young warriors are hot and fiery, and this young Knight, they say, has succeeded to all his brother's favour with the Prince."

"I will not be bearded by a boy," returned Clarenham, thrusting him aside. "Hark you, Sir Eustace. You have been raised to a height which has turned your head, your eyes have been dazzled by the gilding of your spurs, and you have fancied yourself a man; but in your own county and your own family, airs are not to be borne. We rate you at what you are worth, and are not to be imposed on by idle tales which the boastful young men of the Prince's court frame of each other. Give up these pretensions, depart in peace to your fellows at Bordeaux, and we will forget your insolent interference."

"Never, while I live," replied Eustace. "Vassals of Lynwood, guard your young

50

Lord."

"Vassals of Lynwood," said Fulk, "will you see your young Lord carried off to perish in some unknown region, and yourselves left a prey to an adventurer and freebooter?"

"For that matter, my Lord," said an old farmer, "if all tales be true, Master Arthur is like to learn less harm with Sir Eustace than in your jolly household—I for one will stand by our good Lord's brother to the last. What say you, comrades?"

"Hurrah for the Lances of Lynwood!" shouted John Ingram, and the cry was taken up by many a gruff honest voice, till the hall rang again, and the opposing shout of "a Clarenham, a Clarenham!" was raised by the retainers of the Baron. Eustace, at the same moment, raised his nephew in his arms, and lifted him up into the embrasure of one of the high windows. Sir Philip Ashton still hung upon Clarenham, pleading in broken sentences which were lost in the uproar: "Hold! Hold! my Lord. Nay, nay, think but"—(here he was thrust roughly aside by Fulk) —"Sir Eustace, do but hear—it will be a matter for the council—in the name of the King—for the love of Heaven—Leonard, son Leonard! for Heaven's sake what have you to do with the matter? Down with that sword, and follow me! Dost not hear, froward boy? Our names will be called in question! Leonard, on your duty—Ha! have a care! there!"

These last words were broken short, as Gaston, rushing forwards to his master's side, overthrew the table, which carried Sir Philip with it in the fall, and he lay prostrate under the boards, a stumbling-block to a stream of eager combatants, who one after another dashed against him, fell, and either rose again, or remained kicking and struggling with each other.

After several minutes' confused fighting, the tumult cleared away, as it were, leaving the principals on each side opposite to each other, and as the fortune of the day rested on their conflict, all became gradually fixed in attention, resting upon their weapons, in readiness at any moment to renew their own portion of the combat.

Fulk, tall and robust, had far more the appearance of strength than his slenderly-made antagonist, but three years in the school of chivalry had not been wasted by Eustace, and the sword of Du Guesclin was in a hand well accustomed to its use. Old Ralph was uttering under his breath ecstatic exclamations: "Ha! Well struck! A rare foil—a perfect hit—Have a care—Ah! there comes my old blow—That is right—Old Sir Henry's master-stroke— There—one of your new French backstrokes—but it told—Oh! have a care—The Saints guard—Ay— There—Follow it up! Hurrah for Lynwood!" as Fulk tottered, slipped, sank on one knee, and receiving a severe blow on the head with the back of the sword, measured his length on the ground.

"Hurrah for Lynwood!" re-echoed through the hall, but Eustace cut short the clamour at once, by saying, "Peace, my friends, and thanks! Sir Fulk de Clarenham," he added, as his fallen foe moved, and began to raise himself, "you have received a lesson, by which I hope you will profit. Leave the house, whose mourning you have insulted, and thank your relationship that I forbear to bring

51

this outrage to the notice of the King."

While Eustace spoke, Fulk had, by the assistance of two of his retainers, recovered his feet; but though unwounded, he was so dizzied with the blow as to be passive in their hands, and to allow himself to be led into the court, and placed on his horse. Before riding out of the gates, he turned round, and clenching his fist, glanced malignantly at Eustace, and muttered, "You shall aby it."

Another shout of "Down with the false Clarenham! Hurrah for the Lances of Lynwood, and the brave young Knight!" was raised in the court by the peasantry, among whom Fulk was so much hated, that not even regard for their future welfare could prevent them from indulging in this triumph. Probably, too, they expected the satisfaction of drinking the health of the victor, for there were many disappointed countenances when he spoke from the steps of the porch: —"Thanks for your good-will, my friends. Fare ye well, depart in peace, and remember your young Lord." Then turning to the parish Priest, he added, in a low voice, "See that they leave the Castle as soon as possible. The gates must be secured as soon as may be."

He turned back into the hall, and at the door was met by little Arthur, who caught hold of his hand, exclaiming, "So you have won me, and shall keep me forever, Uncle Eustace; but come in, for here is poor old Sir Philip, who was thrown down under the table in the scuffle, bemoaning himself most lamentably."

"Sir Philip hurt?" said Eustace, who, vexed as he was by Sir Philip's behaviour, preserved a certain neighbourly hereditary respect for him; "I trust not seriously," and he advanced towards the arm-chair, where Sir Philip Ashton was sitting, attended by Father Cyril and a man-at-arms, and groaning and complaining of his bruises, while at the same time he ordered the horses to be brought out as speedily as possible.

"Surely," said Eustace, "you should not be in such haste, Sir Philip. I grieve that you should have met with this mishap. But you had better remain here, and try what rest will do for you."

"Remain here!" said Sir Philip, almost shuddering. "Nay, nay, my young Sir, I would not have you to remain here, nor any of us, for longer space than the saddling of a horse. Alas! alas! my young friend, I grieve for you. I loved your father well.—Look from the window, Leonard. Are the horses led forth?"

"But why this haste?" asked Sir Eustace. "You are heavily bruised—best let Father Cyril look to your hurts."

"Thanks, Sir Eustace; but—Ah! my back!—but I would not remain under this roof for more than you could give me. I should but endanger myself without benefiting you. Alas! alas! that I should have fallen upon such a fray! I am sorry for you, my brave youth!"

"I thank you, Sir Philip, but I know not what I have done to deserve your concern."

"Hot blood! wilful blood!" said Sir Philip, shaking his head. "Are the horses come? Here! your hand, Leonard, help me to rise—Ah! ah! not so fast—Oh! I shall never get over it! There—mind you, I did all to prevent this unhappy business—I am clear of it! Fare you well, Sir Eustace—take an old man's advice, give up the boy, and leave the country before worse comes of it."

"What is likely to come of it?" said Eustace; "Clarenham made an uncalled-for, unjust, shameless attempt to seize the person of my ward. I repelled him by force of arms, and I think he would scarce like to call the attention of justice to his own share in the matter."

"Ah! well, you speak boldly, but before you have reached my years, you will have learnt what it is to have for your foe the most mighty man of the county—nay, of the court; for your foe, Lord de Clarenham, is in close friendship with the Earl of Pembroke. Beware, my young friend, beware!"

When the hall was clear of guests, a council was held between the Knight, the Priest, and the two Esquires. Its result was, that Arthur's person, as the most important point, should be secured, by his uncle carrying him at once to the Prince's protection at Bordeaux; but it was only with difficulty that Eustace was prevailed on to fly, as he said, from his accusers. The good Father had to say, with a smile, that after all there was as much need for patience and submission under the helm as under the cowl, before Eustace at length consented. Cyril meanwhile was to lay the case before the Chancellor, William of Wykeham, and Eustace gave him letters to the Duke of Lancaster and to Sir Richard Ferrars, in the hopes of their recommending his suit.

Eustace then received from the hands of the Priest a bag of gold coins, his portion as a younger son, part of which he gave to be distributed in alms, part he still confided to Father Cyril's keeping, and the rest he was to take away for present needs—and they parted for the last night of his brief stay at Lynwood Keep.

CHAPTER X

In the early morning, Sir Eustace and his few followers were in their saddles, little Arthur riding between his uncle and Gaston. The chief part of the day was spent on the journey. They dined, to Arthur's glee, on provisions they had brought with them, seated on a green bank near a stream, and at evening found themselves at the door of a large hostel, its open porch covered by a vine.

The host and his attendants ran out at first to meet them with alacrity, but, on seeing them, appeared disappointed. And as the Knight, dismounting, ordered supper and bed, the host replied that he could indeed engage to find food, and to accommodate their steeds, but that the whole of the inn had been secured on behalf of two noble ladies and their train, who were each moment expected.

"Be it so," said Eustace; "a truss of hay beside our horses, or a settle by the fire, is all we need. Here is a taste already of a warrior's life for you, Arthur."

The boy was delighted, certain that to sleep beside his pony was far more delightful, as well as more manly, than to rest in his bed, like a lady at home.

As this was arranged, a sound of horses' feet approached, and a band of men-at-arms rode up to the door. Arthur started and seized his uncle's hand as he recognized the Clarenham colours and badge, uttering an exclamation of dismay. "Never fear, Arthur," said Eustace, "they come from the way opposite to ours. It is not pursuit. See, it is an escort—there are ladies among them."

"Four!" said Arthur. "Uncle, that tall dame in black must be the Lady Muriel. And surely the white veil tied with rose-colour belongs to kind Cousin Agnes."

"True! These are no Clarenhams to guard against," said Eustace to his Squire, who looked ready for action. "Lady Muriel, the step-mother of the Baron and his sister, is my godmother, and, by birth, a Lynwood."

Then stepping forward, he assisted the elder lady to dismount; she returned his courtesy by a slight inclination, as to a stranger, but her companion, who had lightly sprung to the ground, no sooner perceived him than she exclaimed, "Eustace!" then laying her hand on Lady Muriel's arm, "Mother, it is Sir Eustace Lynwood."

"Ha! my gallant godson!" said the Baroness, greeting him cordially. "Well met, brave youth! No wonder in that knightly figure I did not know my kinswoman's little page. How does my gentle niece, Eleanor?"

"Alack! then you have not heard the tidings?" said Eustace.

"We heard long since she was sick with grief," said Lady Muriel, much alarmed. "What mean you? Is she worse? You weep—surely she still lives!"

"Ah! honoured dame, we come even now from laying her in her grave. Here is her orphan boy."

Young Agnes could not restrain a cry of grief and horror, and trying to repress her weeping till it should be without so many witnesses, Lady Muriel and her bower-woman led her to their apartments in the inn. Eustace was greatly affected by her grief. She had often accompanied her step-mother on visits to Lynwood Keep in the peaceful days of their childhood; she had loved no sport better than to sit listening to his romantic discourses of chivalry, and had found in the shy, delicate, dreamy boy, something congenial to her own quiet nature; and, in short, when Eustace indulged in a vision, Agnes was ever the lady of it, the pale slight Agnes, with no beauty save her large soft brown eyes, that seemed to follow and take in every fancy or thought of his. Agnes was looked down on,—her father thought she would do him little honour,—her brother cared not for her; save for her step-mother she would have met with little fostering attention, and when Eustace saw her set aside and disregarded, his heart had bounded with the thought that when he should lay his trophies at her feet, Agnes would be honoured for his sake. But Eustace's honours had been barren, and he could only look back with a sad heart to the fancies of his youth, when he had deemed Knight-errantry might win the lady of his love.

Eleanor had been one of the few who had known and loved the damsel of Clarenham, and had encouraged her to lay aside her timidity. Agnes wept for her as a sister, and still could hardly restrain her sobs, when Eustace and his nephew were invited to the presence of the ladies to narrate their melancholy tale.

Many tears were shed, and caresses lavished upon the orphan. The ladies asked his destination, and on hearing that he was to be taken to the Prince's court at Bordeaux, Agnes said, "We, too, are bound to the Prince's court. I am to journey thither with Fulk. Were it not better for Arthur to travel with us? Most carefully would we guard him. It would spare him many a hardship, for which he is scarce old enough; and his company would be a solace, almost a protection to me. My pretty playfellow, will you be my travelling companion?"

"I would go with you, Cousin Agnes, for you are kind and gentle, and I love you well; but a brave Knight's son must learn to rough it; and besides, I would not go with Sir Fulk, your brother, for he is a false and cruel Knight, who persecuted my blessed mother to the very death."

"Can this be? O speak, Eustace!" said Agnes. "What means the boy? Hath Fulk shown himself other than a loving kinsman?"

The Baroness, who understood her step-son's character better than did his young sister, and who was informed of the old enmity between the two houses, felt considerable anxiety as to what they were now to hear; when Eustace, beginning, "Ah, Lady, I grieve twice in the day to sadden your heart; yet since so much has been said, it were best to relate the whole truth," proceeded to tell what had passed respecting the wardship of young Arthur. Agnes's eyes filled with burning tears of indignation. "O dear Lady Mother!" cried she, "take me back to our Convent! How can I meet my brother! How conceal my anger and my shame!"

"This is far worse than even I feared," said Lady Muriel. "I knew Fulk to be unscrupulous and grasping, but I did not think him capable of such foul oppression. For you, my sweet Agnes—would that I could prevail on him to leave you in the safe arms of the cloister—but, alas! I have no right to detain you from a brother's guardianship."

"I dreaded this journey much before," said Agnes; "but now, even my trust in Fulk is gone; I shall see round me no one in whom to place confidence. Alas! alas!"

"Nay, fair Agnes," said Eustace, "he will surely be a kind brother to thee—he cannot be otherwise."

"How love and trust when there is no esteem? Oh, Mother, Mother! this is loneliness indeed! In that strange, courtly throng, who will protect and shelter me?"

"There is an Arm—" began the Baroness.

"Yes, noble Lady, there is one arm," eagerly exclaimed Eustace, "that would only deem itself too much honoured if it could be raised in your service."

"I spoke of no arm of flesh," said Lady Muriel, reprovingly—and Eustace hung his head abashed. "I spake of the Guardian who will never be wanting to the orphan."

There was a silence, first broken by Eustace. "One thing there is, that I would fain ask of your goodness," said he: "many a false tale, many a foul slander, will be spoken of me, and many may give heed to them; but let that be as it will, they shall not render my heart heavy while I can still believe that you give no ear to them."

"Sir Eustace," said the Lady of Clarenham, "I have known you from childhood, and it would go hard with me to believe aught dishonourable of the pupil of Sir Reginald and of Eleanor."

"Yes, Sir Eustace," added Agnes, "it would break my heart to distrust you; for then I must needs believe that faith, truth, and honour had left the world."

"And now," said Lady Muriel, who thought the conversation had been sufficiently tender to fulfil all the requirements of the connection of families, and of their old companionship, "now, Agnes, we must take leave of our kind kinsman, since, doubtless, he will desire to renew his journey early to-morrow."

Eustace took the hint, and bent his knee to kiss the hands which were extended to him by the two ladies; then left the room, feeling, among all the clouds which darkened his path, one clear bright ray to warm and gladden his heart. Agnes trusted his truth, Agnes would be at Bordeaux,—he might see her, and she would hear of his deeds.

Agnes, while she wept over her kinswoman's death and her brother's faults, rejoiced in having met her old playfellow, and found him as noble a Knight as her fancy had often pictured him; and in the meanwhile, the good old Lady Muriel sighed to herself, and shook her head at the thought of the sorrows which an attachment would surely cause to these two young creatures.

It was early in the morning that Eustace summoned his nephew from the couch which one of the Clarenham retainers had yielded him, and, mounting their horses, they renewed their journey towards the coast.

Without further adventure, the Lances of Lynwood, as Arthur still chose to call their little party, safely arrived at Rennes, the capital of Brittany, where Jean de Montford held his court. Here they met the tidings that Charles V. had summoned the Prince of Wales to appear at his court, to answer an appeal made against him to the sovereign by the vassals of the Duchy of Aquitaine. Edward's answer was, that he would appear indeed, but that it should be in full armour, with ten thousand Knights and Squires at his back; and the war had already been renewed.

The intelligence added to Eustace's desire to be at Bordeaux, but he could not venture through the enemy's country without exposing himself to death or captivity; and even within the confines of Brittany itself, Duke John, though bound by gratitude and affection to the alliance of the King, who had won for him his ducal coronet, was unable to control the enmity which his subjects bore to the English, and assured the Knight that a safe-conduct from him would only occasion his being robbed and murdered in secret, instead of being taken a prisoner in fair fight and put to ransom.

If Eustace had been alone with his staunch followers, he would have trusted to their good swords and swift steeds; but to place Arthur in such perils would be but to justify Fulk's accusations; and there was no alternative but to accept the offer made to him by Jean de Montford, for the sake of his Duchess, a daughter of Edward III., to remain a guest at his court until the arrival of a sufficient party of English Knights, who were sure to be attracted by the news of the war.

No less than two months was he obliged to wait, during which both he and Gaston chafed grievously under their forced captivity; but at length he learnt that a band of Free Companions had arrived at Rennes, on their way to offer their service to the Prince of Wales; accordingly he set forth, and after some interval found himself once more in the domains of the house of Plantagenet.

It was late in the evening when he rode through the gates of Bordeaux, and sought the abode of the good old Gascon merchant, where he had always lodged. He met with a ready welcome, and inquiring into the most recent news of the town, learnt that the Prince was considered to be slightly improved in health; but that no word was spoken of the army taking the field, and the war was chiefly carried on by the siege of Castles. He asked for Sir John Chandos, and was told that high words had passed between him and the Prince respecting a hearth-tax, and that since he had returned to his government, and seldom or never appeared at the council board. It was the Earl of Pembroke who was all-powerful there. And here the old Gascon wandered into lamentable complaints of the aforesaid hearth-tax, from which Eustace could scarcely recall him to answer whether the English Baron de Clarenham had arrived at Bordeaux. He had come, and with as splendid a train as ever was beheld, and was in high favour at court.

This was no pleasing intelligence, but Eustace determined to go the next day to present his nephew to the Prince immediately after the noontide meal, when it was the wont of the Plantagenet Princes to throw their halls open to their subjects.

Accordingly, leading Arthur by the hand, and attended by Gaston, he made his appearance in the hall just as the banquet was concluded, but ere the Knights had dispersed. Many well-known faces were there, but as he advanced up the space between the two long tables, he was amazed at meeting scarce one friendly glance of recognition; some looked unwilling to seem to know him, and returned his salutation with distant coldness; others gazed at the window, or were intent on their wine, and of these was Leonard Ashton, whom to his surprise he saw seated among the Knights.

Thus he passed on until he had nearly reached the dais where dined the Prince and the personages of the most exalted rank. Here he paused as his anxious gaze fell upon the Prince, and marked his countenance and mien—alas! how changed! He sat in his richly-carved chair, wrapped in a velvet mantle, which, even on that bright day of a southern spring, he drew closer round him with a shuddering chilliness. His elbow rested on the arm of his chair, and his wasted cheek leant on his hand—the long thin fingers of which showed white and transparent as a lady's; his eyes were bent on the ground, and a look of suffering or of moody thought hung over the whole of that face, once full of free and open cheerfulness. Tears filled Eustace's eyes as he beheld that wreck of manhood and thought of that bright day of hope and gladness when his brother had presented him to the Prince.

As he hesitated to advance, the Prince, raising his eyes, encountered that earnest and sorrowful gaze, but only responding by a stern glance of displeasure. Eustace, however, stepped forward, and bending one knee, said, "My Lord, I come to report myself as returned to your service, and at the same time to crave for my nephew the protection you were graciously pleased to promise him."

"It is well, Sir Eustace Lynwood," said Edward, coldly, and with a movement of his head, as if to dismiss him from his presence; "and you, boy, come hither," he added as Arthur, seeing his uncle rise and retreat a few steps, was following his example. "I loved your father well," he said, laying his hand on the boy's bright

57

wavy hair, "and you shall find in me a steady friend as long as you prove yourself not unworthy of the name you bear."

In spite of the awe with which Arthur felt his head pressed by that royal hand, in spite of his reverence for the hero and the Prince, he raised his eyes and looked upon the face of the Prince with an earnest, pleading, almost upbraiding gaze, as if, child as he was, he deprecated the favour, which so evidently marked the slight shown to his uncle. But the Prince did not heed him, and rising from his chair, said, "Thine arm, Clarenham. Let us to the Princess, and present her new page. Follow me, boy."

With a wistful look at his uncle, standing alone on the step of the dais, Arthur reluctantly followed the Prince as, leaning on Clarenham's arm, he left the hall, and, crossing a gallery, entered a large apartment. At one end was a canopy embroidered with the arms and badges of the heir of England, and beneath it were two chairs of state, one of which was occupied by Joan Plantagenet, Princess of Wales, once the Fair Maid of Kent, and though now long past her youth, still showing traces of beauty befitting the lady for whom her royal cousin had displayed such love and constancy.

As her husband entered, she rose, and looking anxiously at him, while she came forward to meet him, inquired whether he felt fatigued. "No, my fair dame," replied the Prince, "I came but to present you your new page; the young cousin, respecting whose safety my Lord de Clarenham hath been so much in anxiety."

"Then it is his uncle who hath brought him?" asked Joan.

"Yes," replied Edward, "he himself brought him to the hall, and even had the presumption to claim the protection for him that I pledged to his father, when I deemed far otherwise of this young Eustace."

"What account does he give of the length of time that he has spent on the road?" asked the Princess.

"Ay, there is the strangest part of the tale," said Fulk Clarenham, with a sneer, "since he left the poor simple men at Lynwood believing that he was coming at full speed to seek my Lord the Prince's protection for the child, a convenient excuse for eluding the inquiries of justice into his brawls at the funeral, as well as for the rents which he carried off with him; but somewhat inconsistent when it is not for five months that he makes his appearance at Bordeaux, and then in the society of a band of *routiers*."

"It shall be inquired into," said the Prince.

"Nay, nay, my Lord," said Fulk, "may I pray you of your royal goodness to press the matter no further. He is still young, and it were a pity to cast dishonour on a name which has hitherto been honourable. Since my young cousin is safe, I would desire no more, save to guard him from his future machinations. For his brother's sake, my Lord, I would plead with you."

"Little did I think such things of him," said the Prince, "when I laid knighthood on his shoulder in the battle-field of Navaretta; yet I remember even then old Chandos chid me for over-hastiness. Poor old Chandos, he has a rough tongue, but a true heart!"

"And, under favour, I would say," answered Clarenham, "that it might have been those early-won honours that turned the head of such a mere youth, so entirely without guidance, or rather, with the guidance of that dissolute Squire, who, I grieve to observe, still haunts his footsteps. Knighthood, with nought to maintain it, is, in truth, a snare."

"Well, I am weary of the subject," said the Prince, leaning back in his chair. "The boy is safe, and, as you say, Fulk, that is all that is of importance. Call hither the troubadour that was in the hall at noon. I would have your opinion of his lay," he added, turning to his wife.

The indignation may be imagined with which Arthur listened to this conversation, as he stood on the spot to which Edward had signed to him to advance, when he presented him to the Princess. He longed ardently to break in with an angry refutation of the slanders cast on his uncle, but he was too well trained in the rules of chivalry, to say nothing of the awful respect with which he regarded the Prince, to attempt to utter a word, and he could only edge himself as far away as was possible from Clarenham, and cast at him glances of angry reproach.

His uneasy movements were interpreted as signs of fatigue and impatience of restraint by one of the ladies, who was sitting at no great distance, a very beautiful and graceful maiden, the Lady Maude Holland, daughter to the Princess of Wales, by her first marriage; and she kindly held out her hand to him, saying, "Come hither, my pretty page. You have not learnt to stand stiff and straight, like one of the supporters of a coat-of-arms. Come hither, and let me lead you to company better suited to your years."

Arthur came willingly, as there was no more to hear about his uncle; and besides, it was away from the hateful Clarenham. She led him across the hall to a tall arched doorway, opening upon a wide and beautiful garden, filled with the plants and shrubs of the south of France, and sloping gently down to the broad expanse of the blue waves of the Garonne. She looked round on all sides, and seeing no one, made a few steps forward on the greensward, then called aloud, "Thomas!" no answer, "Edward! Harry of Lancaster!" but still her clear silvery voice was unheeded, until a servant came from some other part of the building, and, bowing, awaited her orders. "Where are Lord Edward and the rest?" she asked.

"Gone forth," the servant believed, "to ride on the open space near St. Ursula's Convent."

"None left at home?"

"None, noble Lady."

"None," repeated Lady Maude, "save the little Lord Richard, whose baby company your pageship would hardly esteem. You must try to endure the quietness of the lady's chamber, unless you would wish to be at once introduced to the grave master of the Damoiseaux."

At this moment Arthur's eye fell upon a lady who had just emerged from a long shady alley, up which she had been slowly walking, and the bright look of recognition which lighted up his face, was so different from the shy and constrained expression he had hitherto worn, that Lady Maude remarked it, and

59

following his gaze, said, "Lady Agnes de Clarenham? Ah yes, she is of kin to you. Let us go meet her." Then, as they approached, she said, "Here, Agnes, I have brought you a young cousin of yours, whom the Prince has just conducted into my mother's chamber, where he bore so rueful a countenance that I grew pitiful enough to come forth on a bootless errand after his fellow Damoiseaux, who, it seems, are all out riding. So I shall even leave him to you, for there is a troubadour in the hall, whose lay I greatly long to hear."

Away tripped Lady Maude, well pleased to be free from the burthen her good-nature had imposed on her.

"Arthur," exclaimed Agnes, "what joy to see you! Is your uncle here?"

"Yes," said Arthur, "but oh, Cousin Agnes! if you had been by to hear the foul slanders which Sir Fulk has been telling the Prince—oh, Agnes! you would disown him for your brother."

"Arthur," said Agnes, with a voice almost of anguish, "how could he—why did he tarry so long on the road?"

"How could we come on when the Duke of Brittany himself said it was certain death or captivity? We were forced to wait for an escort. And now, Agnes, think of your brother saying that Uncle Eustace carried off the rents of Lynwood, when every man in the Castle could swear it was only the money Father Cyril had in keeping for his inheritance."

"Alas!" said Agnes.

"And the Prince will believe it—the Prince looks coldly on him already, and my uncle loves the Prince like his own life. Oh, he will be ready to die with grief! Agnes! Agnes! what is to be done? But you don't believe it!" he proceeded, seeing that she was weeping bitterly. "You do not believe it—you promised you never would! Oh say you do not believe it!"

"I do not, Arthur; I never believed half they said of him; but oh, that long delay was a sore trial to my confidence, and cruelly confirmed their tales."

"And think of Fulk, too, hindering the Prince from inquiring, because he says he would spare my uncle for my father's sake, when the truth is, he only fears that the blackness of his own designs should be seen! And Gaston, too, he slandered. Oh, Agnes! Agnes! that there should be such wickedness, and we able to do nought!"

"Nought but weep and pray!" said Agnes. "And yet I can bear it better now that you are here. Your presence refutes the worst accusation, and removes a heavy weight from my mind."

"You distrust him too! I cannot love you if you do."

"Never, never! I only feared some evil had befallen you, and grieved to see the use made of your absence. Your coming should make my heart light again."

"Shall I often see you, Cousin Agnes? for there is none else in this wide Castle that I shall care for."

"Oh yes, Arthur, there are full twenty pages little older than yourself—Lord Thomas Holland, the Prince's stepson, brother to the lady that led you to me; little Piers de Greilly, nephew to the Captal de Buch; young Lord Henry of Lancaster; and the little Prince Edward himself. You will have no lack of merry playmates."

"Ah, but to whom can I talk of my blessed mother and of Uncle Eustace, and of Lynwood Keep, and poor old Blanc Etoile, that I promised Ralph I would bear in mind?"

"Well, Arthur," said Agnes, cheerfully, "it is the pages' duty to wait on the ladies in hall and bower, and the ladies' office to teach them all courtly manners, and hear them read and say the Credo and Ave. You shall be my own especial page and servant. Is it agreed?"

"Oh yes," said the boy. "I wonder if the master of the Damoiseaux is as strict as that lady said, and I wonder when I shall see Uncle Eustace again."

CHAPTER XI

If Arthur Lynwood felt desolate when he left his uncle's side, it was not otherwise with Sir Eustace as he lost sight of the child, who had so long been his charge, and who repaid his anxiety with such confiding affection. The coveted fame, favour, and distinction seemed likewise to have deserted him. The Prince's coldness hung heavily on him, and as he cast his eyes along the ranks of familiar faces, not one friendly look cheered him. His greetings were returned with coldness, and a grave haughty courtesy was the sole welcome. Chafed and mortified, he made a sign to Gaston, and they were soon in the street once more.

"Coward clown!" burst forth Gaston at once. "Would that I could send all his grinning teeth down the false throat of him!"

"Whose? What mean you?"

"Whose but that sulky recreant, Ashton? He has done well to obtain knighthood, or I would beat him within an inch of his life with my halbert, and if he dared challenge me, slay him as I would a carrion crown! He a Knight! Thanks to his acres and to Lord Pembroke!"

"Patience, patience, Gaston—I have not yet heard of what he accuses me."

"No! he has learnt policy—he saith it not openly! He would deny it, as did his Esquire when I taxed him with it! Would that you could not tell a letter! Sir Eustace, of your favour let me burn every one of your vile books."

"My innocent friends! Nay, nay, Gaston—they are too knightly to merit such measure. Then it is the old accusation of witchcraft, I suppose. So I was in league with the Castilian witch and her cats, was I?"

"Ay; and her broom-stick or her cats wafted you to Lynwood, where you suddenly stood in the midst of the mourners, borne into the hall on a howling blast! How I got there, I am sorry to say, the craven declared not, lest I should give him the lie at once!"

"But surely, such a tale is too absurd and vulgar to deceive our noble Prince."

"Oh, there is another version for his ears. This is only for the lower sort, who might not have thought the worse of you for kidnapping your nephew, vowing his mother should remain unburied till he was in your hands, and carrying off all his rents."

"That is Clarenham's slander."

61

"Yes."

"And credited by the Prince? Oh! little did I think the hand which laid knighthood on my shoulder should repent the boon that it gave!" exclaimed Eustace, with a burst of sorrow rather than anger.

"Do you not challenge the traitor at once?"

"I trow not, unless he speaks the charge to my face. Father Cyril declared that any outbreak on my part would damage our cause in the eyes of the Chancellor; we must bide our time. Since Arthur is safe, I will bear my own burden. I am guiltless in this matter, and I trust that the blessing of Heaven on my deeds shall restore a name, obscured, but not tarnished."

The resolution to forbear was tested, for time passed on without vindicating him. With such art had the toils of his enemies been spread, that no opening was left him for demanding an explanation. The calumnies could only be brought home to the lowest retainers of Clarenham and Ashton, and the only result of the zealous refutation by the followers of Sir Eustace was a brawl between John Ingram and a yeoman of Clarenham's, ending in their spending a week in the custody of the Provost Marshal.

Had there been any tournament or like sport at Bordeaux, Eustace could have asserted his place, and challenged the attention of the court; but the state of the Prince's health prevented such spectacles; nor had he any opportunity of acquiring honour by his deeds in arms. No army took the field on either side, and the war was chiefly carried on by expeditions for the siege or relief of frontier castles; and here his unusual rank as Knight Banneret stood in his way, since it was contrary to etiquette for him to put himself under the command of a Knight Bachelor. He was condemned therefore to a weary life of inaction, the more galling, because his poverty made it necessary to seek maintenance as formerly at the Prince's table, where he was daily reminded, by the altered demeanour of his acquaintance, of the unjust suspicions beneath which he laboured. He had hoped that a dismissal from his post in the Prince's band would give him the much-desired opportunity of claiming a hearing, but he was permitted to receive his pay and allowance as usual, and seemed completely overlooked. It was well that Gaston's gay temper could not easily be saddened by their circumstances, and his high spirits and constant attachment often cheered his Knight in their lonely evenings. Eustace had more than once striven to persuade him to forsake his failing fortunes; but to this the faithful Squire would never consent, vowing that he was as deeply implicated in all their accusations as Sir Eustace himself; and who would wish to engage a fellow-servant of the black cats! There were two others whom Eustace would fain believe still confided in his truth and honour, his nephew Arthur, and Lady Agnes de Clarenham; but he never saw them, and often his heart sank at the thought of the impression that the universal belief might make on the minds of both. And to add to his depression, a rumour prevailed throughout Bordeaux that the Baron of Clarenham had promised his sister's hand to Sir Leonard Ashton.

Nearly a year had passed since Eustace had left England, and his situation continued unchanged. Perhaps the Prince regarded him with additional displeasure, since news had arrived that Sir Richard Ferrars had made application to the Duke of Lancaster to interest the King in the cause of the guardianship; for there was, at this time, a strong jealousy, in the mind of the Prince, of the mighty power and influence of John of Gaunt, which he already feared might be used to the disadvantage of his young sons.

The cause was, at length, decided, and a letter from good Father Cyril conveyed to Eustace the intelligence that the Chancellor, William of Wykeham, Bishop of Winchester, having given due weight to Sir Reginald's dying words and Lady Lynwood's testament, had pronounced Sir Eustace Lynwood the sole guardian of the person and estate of his nephew, and authorized all the arrangements he had made on his departure.

Affairs altogether began to wear a brighter aspect. The first indignation against Sir Eustace had subsided, and he was treated, in general, with indifference rather than marked scorn. The gallant old Chandos was again on better terms with the Prince, and, coming to Bordeaux, made two or three expeditions, in which Eustace volunteered to join, and gained some favourable, though slight, notice from the old Knight. Fulk Clarenham, too, having received from the Prince the government of Perigord, was seldom at court, and no active enemy appeared to be at work against him.

Agnes de Clarenham, always retiring and pensive, and seldom sought out by those who admired gayer damsels, was sitting apart in the embrasure of a window, whence, through an opening in the trees of the garden, she could catch a distant glimpse of the blue waters of the river where it joined the sea, which separated her from her native land, and from her who had ever been as a mother to her. She was so lost in thought, that she scarce heard a step approaching, till the unwelcome sound of "Fair greeting to you, Lady Agnes" caused her to look up and behold the still more unwelcome form of Sir Leonard Ashton. To escape from him was the first idea, for his clownish manners, always unpleasant to her, had become doubly so, since he had presumed upon her brother's favour to offer to her addresses from which she saw no escape; and with a brief reply of "Thanks for your courtesy, Sir Knight," she was about to rise and mingle with the rest of the party, when he proceeded, bluntly, "Lady Agnes, will you do me a favour?"

"I know of no favour in my power," said she.

"Nay," he said, "it is easily done, and it is as much to your brother as to myself. It is a letter which, methinks, Fulk would not have read out of the family, of which I may call myself one," and he gave a sort of smirk at Agnes;—"but he writes so crabbedly, that I, for one, cannot read two lines,—and I would not willingly give it to a clerk, who might be less secret. So methought, as 'twas the Baron's affair, I would even bring it here, and profit by your Convent-breeding, Lady Agnes."

Agnes took the letter, and began to read:—

"For the hand of the Right Noble and Worshipful Knight, Sir Leonard Ashton, at the court of my Lord the Prince of Wales, these:—

63

"Fair Sir, and brother-in-arms—I hereby do you to wit, that the affair whereof we spoke goes well. Both my Lord of Pembroke, and Sir John Chandos, readily undertook to move the Prince to grant the Banneret you wot of the government of the Castle, and as he hath never forgotten the love he once bore to his brother, he will the more easily be persuaded. Of the garrison we are sure, and all that is now needful is, that the one-eyed Squire, whereof you spoke to me, should receive warning before he arrives at the Castle.

"Tell him to choose his time, and manage matters so that there may be no putting to ransom. He will understand my meaning.

"Greeting you well, therefore,

"Fulk, Baron of Clarenham."

"What means this?" exclaimed Agnes, as a tissue of treachery opened before her eyes.

"Ay, that you may say," said Leonard, his slow brain only fixed upon Fulk's involved sentences, and utterly unconscious of the horror expressed in her tone. "How is a man to understand what he would have me to do? Send to Le Borgne Basque at Chateau Norbelle? Is that it? Read it to me once again, Lady, for the love of the Saints. What am I to tell Le Borgne Basque? No putting to ransom, doth he say? He might be secure enough for that matter—Eustace Lynwood is little like to ransom himself."

"But what mean you?" said Agnes, eagerly hoping that she had done her brother injustice in her first horrible thought. "Sir Eustace Lynwood, if you spake of him, is no prisoner, but is here at Bordeaux."

"He shall not long be so," said Leonard. "Heard you not this very noon that the Prince bestows on him the government of Chateau Norbelle on the marches of Gascony? Well, that is the matter treated of in this letter. Let me see, let me see, how was it to be? Yes, that is it! It is Le Borgne Basque who is Seneschal. Ay, true, that I know,—and 'twas he who was to admit Clisson's men."

"Admit Clisson's men!"

"Ay—'tis one of those Castles built by the old Paladin, Renaud de Montauban, that Eustace used to talk about. I ween he did not know of this trick that will be played on himself—and all of them have, they say, certain secret passages leading through the vaults into the Castle. Le Borgne Basque knows them all, for he has served much in those parts, and Fulk placed him as Seneschal for the very purpose."

"For the purpose of admitting Clisson's men? Do I understand you right, Sir Knight, or do my ears play me false?"

"Yes, I speak right. Do you not see, Lady Agnes, it is the only way to free your house of this stumbling-block—this beggarly upstart Eustace—who, as long as he lives, will never acknowledge Fulk's rights, and would bring up his nephew to the same pride."

"And is it possible, Sir Leonard, that brother of mine, and belted Knight, should devise so foul a scheme of treachery! Oh, unsay it again! Let me believe it was my own folly that conjured up so monstrous a thought!"

"Ay, that is the way with women," said Leonard; "they never look at the sense of the matter. Why, this Eustace, what terms should be kept with him, who has dealings with the Evil One? and—"

"I will neither hear a noble Knight maligned, nor suffer him to be betrayed," interrupted Agnes. "I have listened to you too long, Sir Leonard Ashton, and will stain my ears no longer. I thank you, however, for having given me such warning as to enable me to traverse them."

"What will you do?" asked Leonard, with a look of impotent anger.

"Appeal instantly to the Prince. Tell him the use that is made of his Castles, and the falsehoods told him of his most true-hearted Knight!" and Agnes, with glancing eyes, was already rising for the purpose, forgetting, in her eager indignation, all that must follow, when Leonard, muttering "What madness possessed me to tell her!" stood full before her, saying, gloomily, "Do so, Lady, if you choose to ruin your brother!" The timid girl stood appalled, as the horrible consequences of such an accusation arose before her.

That same day Eustace was summoned to the Prince's presence.

"Sir Eustace Lynwood," said Edward, gravely, "I hear you have served the King well beneath the banner of Sir John Chandos. Your friends have wrought with me to give you occasion to prove yourself worthy of your spurs, and I have determined to confer on you the government of my Chateau of Norbelle, on the frontier of Gascony, trusting to find you a true and faithful governor and Castellane."

"I trust, my Lord, that you have never had occasion to deem less honourably of me," said Eustace; and his clear open eye and brow courted rather than shunned the keen look of scrutiny that the Prince fixed upon him. His heart leapt at the hope that the time for inquiry was come, but the Prince in another moment sank his eyes again, with more, however, of the weary impatience of illness than of actual displeasure, and merely replied, "Kneel down, then, Sir Knight, and take the oaths of fidelity."

Eustace obeyed, hardly able to suppress a sigh at the disappointment of his hopes.

"You will receive the necessary orders and supplies from Sir John Chandos, and from the Treasurer," said Edward, in a tone that intimated the conclusion of the conference; and Eustace quitted his presence, scarce knowing whether to be rejoiced or dissatisfied.

The former, Gaston certainly was. "I have often been heartily weary of garrison duty," said he, "but never can I be more weary of aught, than of being looked upon askance by half the men I meet. And we may sometimes hear the lark sing too, as well as the mouse squeak, Sir Eustace. I know every pass of my native county, and the herds of Languedoc shall pay toll to us."

Sir John Chandos, as Constable of Aquitaine, gave him the requisite orders and information. The fortifications, he said, were in good condition, and the garrison already numerous; but a sum of money was allotted to him in order to increase their numbers as much as he should deem advisable, since it was not improbable that he might have to sustain a siege, as Oliver de Clisson was threatening that part of the frontier. Four days were allowed for his preparations, after which he was to depart for his government.

Eustace was well pleased with all that he heard, and returned to his lodging, where, in the evening twilight, he was deeply engaged in consultation with Gaston, on the number of followers to be raised, when a light step was heard hastily approaching, and Arthur, darting into the room, flung himself on his neck, exclaiming, "Uncle! uncle! go not to this Castle!"

"Arthur, what brings you here? What means this? No foolish frolic, no escape from punishment, I trust?" said Eustace, holding him at some little distance, and fixing his eyes on him intently.

"No, uncle, no! On the word of a true Knight's son," said the boy, stammering, in his eagerness, "believe me, trust me, dear uncle—and go not to this fearful Castle. It is a trap—a snare laid to be your death, by the foulest treachery!"

"Silence, Arthur!" said the Knight, sternly. "Know you not what treason you speak? Some trick has been played on your simplicity, and yet you—child as you are—should as soon think shame of your own father as of the Prince, the very soul of honour."

"Oh, it is not the Prince: he knows nought of it; it is those double traitors, the Baron of Clarenham and Sir Leonard Ashton, who have worked upon him and deceived him."

"Oh, ho!" said Gaston. "The story now begins to wear some semblance of probability."

Arthur turned, looking perplexed. "Master d'Aubricour," said he, "I forgot that you were here. This is a secret which should have been for my uncle's ears alone."

"Is it so?" said Gaston; "then I will leave the room, if it please you and the Knight—though methought I was scarce small enough to be so easily overlooked; and having heard the half—"

"You had best hear the whole," said Arthur. "Uncle Eustace, what think you?"

"I know not what to think, Arthur. You must be your own judge."

Arthur's young brow wore a look of deep thought; at last he said, "Do not go then, Gaston. If I have done wrong, I must bear the blame, and, be it as it may, my uncle needs must tell you all that I may tell him."

"Let us hear, then," said Eustace.

"Well, then," said Arthur, who had by this time collected himself, "you must know that this Chateau Norbelle is one of those built by that famous Paladin, the chief of freebooters, Sir Renaud de Montauban, of whom you have told me so many tales. Now all of these have secret passages in the vaults communicating with the outer country."

"The boy is right," said Gaston; "I have seen one of them in the Castle of Montauban itself."

"Then it seems," proceeded Arthur, "that this Castle hath hitherto been in the keeping of a certain one-eyed Seneschal, a great friend and comrade of Sir Leonard Ashton—"

"Le Borgne Basque!" exclaimed both Knight and Squire, looking at each other in amaze.

"True, true," said Arthur. "Now you believe me. Well, the enemy being in the neighbourhood, it was thought right to increase the garrison, and place it under the command of a Knight, and these cowardly traitors have wrought with my Lord of Pembroke and Sir John Chandos to induce the Prince to give you this post—it being their intention that this wicked Seneschal and his equally wicked garrison should admit Sir Oliver de Clisson, the butcher of Bretagne himself, through the secret passage. And, uncle," said the boy, pressing Eustace's hand, while tears of indignation sprang to his eyes, "the letter expressly said there was to be no putting to ransom. Oh, Uncle Eustace, go not to this Castle!"

"And how came you by this knowledge?" asked the Knight.

"That I may never tell," said Arthur.

"By no means which might not beseem the son of a brave man?" said Eustace.

"Mistrust me not so foully," said the boy. "I know it from a sure hand, and there is not dishonour, save on the part of those villain traitors. Oh, promise me, fair uncle, not to put yourself in their hands!"

"Arthur, I have taken the oaths to the Prince as Castellane. I cannot go back from my duty, nor give up its defence for any cause whatsoever."

"Alas! alas!"

"There would be only one way of avoiding it," said Eustace, "and you must yourself say, Arthur, whether that is open to me. To go to the Prince, and tell him openly what use is made of his Castles, and impeach the villains of their treachery."

"That cannot be," said Arthur, shaking his head sadly—"it is contrary to the pledge I gave for you and for myself. But go not, go not, uncle. Remember, uncle, if you will not take thought for yourself, that you are all that is left me—all that stands between me and that wicked Clarenham.—Gaston, persuade him."

"Gaston would never persuade me to disgrace my spurs for the sake of danger," replied Eustace. "Have you no better learnt the laws of chivalry in the Prince's household, Arthur? Besides, remember old Ralph's proverb, 'Fore-warned is fore-armed.' Think you not that Gaston, and honest Ingram, and I may not be a match for a dozen cowardly traitors? Besides which, see here the gold allotted me to raise more men, with which I will obtain some honest hearts for my defence—and it will go hard with me if I cannot find Sir Renaud's secret door."

"Then, if you will go, uncle, take, take me with you—I could, at least, watch the door; and I know how to hit a mark with a cross-bow as well as Lord Harry of Lancaster himself."

"Take you, Master Arthur? What! steal away the Prince's page that I have been at such pains to bring hither, and carry him to a nest of traitors! Why, it would be the very way to justify Clarenham's own falsehoods."

"And of the blackest are they!" said Arthur. "Think, uncle, of my standing by to hear him breathing his poison to the Prince, and the preventing him from searching to find out the truth, by pretending a regard for my father's name, and your character. Oh that our noble Prince should be deluded by such a recreant, and think scorn of such a Knight as you!"

"I trust yet to prove to him that it is a delusion," said Eustace. "Many a Knight at twenty-two has yet to make his name and fame. Mine, thanks to Du Guesclin and the Prince himself, is already made, and though clouded for a time, with the grace of our Lady and of St. Eustace, I will yet clear it; so, Arthur, be not downcast for me, but think what Father Cyril hath taught concerning evil report and good report. But tell me, how came you hither?"

"She—that is, the person that warned me—let me down from the window upon the head of the great gurgoyle, and from thence I scrambled down by the vines on the wall, ran through the court without being seen by the Squires and grooms, and found my way to the bridge, where happily I met John Ingram, who brought me hither."

"She?" repeated Gaston, with a sly look in his black eyes.

"I have said too much," said Arthur, colouring deeply; "I pray you to forget."

"Forget!" proceeded the Squire, "that is sooner said than done. We shall rack our brains to guess what lady can—"

"Hush, Gaston," said Eustace, as his nephew looked at him imploringly, "tempt not the boy. And you, Arthur, must return to the palace immediately."

"Oh, uncle!" said the boy, "may I not stay with you this one night? It is eight weary months since I have ever seen you, save by peering down through the tall balusters of the Princess's balcony, when the Knights were going to dinner in the hall, and I hoped you would keep me with you at least one night. See how late and dark it is—the Castle gates will be closed by this time."

"It does indeed rejoice my heart to have you beside me, fair nephew," said Eustace, "and yet I know not how to favour such an escape as this, even for such a cause."

"I never broke out of bounds before," said Arthur, "and never will, though Lord Harry and Lord Thomas Holland have more than once asked me to join them."

"Then," said the Knight, "since it is, as you say, too late to rouse the palace, I will take you back in my hand to-morrow morn, see the master of the Damoiseaux, and pray him to excuse you for coming to see me ere my departure."

"Yes, that will be all well," said Arthur; "I could, to be sure, find the corner where Lord Harry has loosened the stones, and get in by the pages' window, ere old Master Michael is awake in the morn; but I think such doings are more like those of a fox than of a brave boy, and though I should be well punished, I will walk in at the door, and hold up my head boldly."

"Shall you be punished then?" said Gaston. "Is your old master of the Damoiseaux very severe?"

"He has not been so hitherto with me," said Arthur: "he scolds me for little, save what you too are displeased with, Master d'Aubricour, because I cannot bring my mouth to speak your language in your own fashion. It is Lord Harry that chiefly falls under his displeasure. But punished now I shall assuredly be, unless Uncle Eustace can work wonders."

"I will see what may be done, Arthur," said Eustace. "And now, have you supped?"

The evening passed off very happily to the little page, who, quite reassured by his uncle's consolations, only thought of the delight of being with one who seemed to supply to him the place at once of an elder brother and of a father.

Early the next morning, Eustace walked with him to the palace. Just before he reached it, he made this inquiry, "Arthur, do you often see the Lady Agnes de Clarenham?"

"Oh, yes, I am with her almost every afternoon. She hears me read, she helps me with my French words, and teaches me courtly manners. I am her own page and servant—but, here we are. This is the door that leads to the room of Master Michael de Sancy, the master of the Damoiseaux."

CHAPTER XII

The next few days were spent in taking precautions against the danger intimated by the mysterious message. Gaston gathered together a few of the ancient Lances of Lynwood, who were glad to enlist under the blue crosslet, and these, with some men-at-arms, who had recently come to Bordeaux to seek employment, formed a body with whom Eustace trusted to be able to keep the disaffected in check. Through vineyards and over gently swelling hills did their course lead them, till, on the evening of the second day's journey, the view to the south was shut in by more lofty and bolder peaks, rising gradually towards the Pyrenees, and on the summit of a rock overhanging a small rapid stream appeared the tall and massive towers of a Castle, surmounted by the broad red cross of St. George, and which their guide pronounced to be the Chateau Norbelle.

"A noble eyrie!" said Eustace, looking up and measuring it with his eye. "Too noble to be sacrificed to the snaring of one poor Knight."

"Shame that such a knightly building should serve for such a nest of traitors!" said Gaston. "Saving treachery, a dozen boys could keep it against a royal host, provided they had half the spirit of your little nephew."

"Let us summon the said traitors," said Eustace, blowing a blast on his bugle. The gates were thrown wide open, the drawbridge lowered, and beneath the portcullis stood the Seneschal, his bunch of keys at his girdle. Both Eustace and Gaston cast searching glances upon him, and his aspect made them for a moment doubt the truth of the warning. A patch covered the lost eye, his moustache was shaved, his hair appeared many shades lighter, as well as his beard, which had been carefully trimmed, and altogether the obsequious Seneschal presented a strong contrast to the dissolute reckless man-at-arms. The Knight debated with himself, whether to let him perceive that he was recognized; and deciding to watch his conduct, he asked by what name to address him.

"Thibault Sanchez," replied Le Borgne Basque, giving his real name, which he might safely do, as it was not known to above two men in the whole Duchy of Aquitaine. "Thibault Sanchez, so please you, noble Sir, a poor Squire from the mountains, who hath seen some few battles and combats in his day, but never one equal to the fight of Najara, where your deeds of prowess—"

"My deeds of prowess, Sir Seneschal, had better rest in silence until our horses have been disposed of, and I have made the rounds of the Castle before the light fails us."

"So late, Sir Knight! and after a long and weary journey? Surely you will drink a cup of wine, and take a night's rest first, relying on me, who, though I be a plain man, trust I understand somewhat of the duties of mine office."

"I sleep not until I have learnt what is committed to my charge," replied the Knight. "Lead the way, Master Sanchez."

"Ah! there is what it is to have a Knight of fame," cried Le Borgne Basque. "What vigilance! what earnestness! Ah, this will be, as I told my comrades even now, the very school of chivalry, the pride of the country."

They had by this time crossed the narrow court, and passing beneath a second portcullised door defended on either side by high battlement walls, nearly double as thick as the steps themselves were wide. At the head was an arched door, heavily studded with nails, and opening into the Castle hall, a gloomy, vaulted room, its loop-hole windows, in their mighty depth of wall, affording little light. A large wood fire was burning in the hearth, and its flame cast a bright red light on some suits of armour that were hung at one end of the hall, as well as on some benches, and a long table in the midst, where were placed some trenchers, drinking horns, and a flask or two of wine.

"A drop of wine, noble Knight," said the Seneschal. "Take a cup to recruit you after your journey, and wash the dust from your throat."

A long ride in full armour beneath the sun of Gascony made this no unacceptable proposal, but the probability that the wine might be drugged had been contemplated by Eustace, who had not only resolved to abstain himself, but had exacted the same promise from d'Aubricour, sorely against his will.

"We will spare your flasks till a time of need," said Eustace, only accepting the basin of fair water presented to him to lave his hands. "And now to the walls," he added, after he had filled a cup with water from the pitcher and refreshed himself with it. Gaston followed his example, not without a wistful look at the wine, and Sanchez was obliged to lead the way up a long flight of spiral steps to two other vaulted apartments, one over the other—the lower destined for the sleeping chamber of the Knight and his Squire, the higher for such of the men-at-arms as could not find accommodation in the hall, or in the offices below. Above this they came out on the lead-covered roof, surrounded with a high crenellated stone parapet, where two or three warders were stationed. Still higher rose one small octagonal watch-tower, on the summit of which was planted a spear bearing St. George's pennon, and by its side Sir Eustace now placed his own.

This done, Eustace could not help standing for a few moments to look forth upon the glorious expanse of country beneath him—the rich fields and fair vineyards spreading far away to the west and north, with towns and villages here and there rising among them; while far away to the east, among higher hills, lay the French town of Carcassonne, a white mass, just discernible by the light of the setting sun; and the south was bounded by the peaks of the Pyrenees, amongst which lay all Eustace's brightest recollections of novelty, adventure, and hopes of glory.

Descending the stairs once more, after traversing the hall, they found themselves in the kitchen, where a large supper was preparing. Here, too, was the buttery, some other small chambers fit for storehouses, and some stalls for horses, all protected by the great bartizan at the foot of the stairs, which was capable of being defended even after the outer court was won. By the time the new-comers had made themselves acquainted with these localities, the evening was fast closing in, and Sanchez pronounced that the Knight's survey was concluded in good time for supper.

"I have not yet seen the vaults," said Eustace.

"The vaults, Sir Knight! what would you see there, save a few rusted chains, and some whitened bones, that have been there ever since the days of the Count de Montfort and the heretic Albigenses! They say that their accursed spirits haunt the place."

"I have heard," returned Sir Eustace, "that these Castles of Gascony are said to have secret passages communicating with their vaults, and I would willingly satisfy my own eyes that we are exposed to no such peril here."

"Nay, not a man in the Castle will enter those vaults after sunset, Sir Knight. The Albigenses, Sir Eustace!"

"I will take the risk alone," said Eustace. "Hand me a torch there!"

Gaston took another, and Thibault Sanchez, seeing them so resolute, chose to be of the party. The torches shed their red glare over the stone arches on which the Castle rested, and there was a chill damp air and earthy smell, which made both Knight and Squire shudder and start. No sooner had they entered than Thibault, trembling exclaimed, in a tone of horror, "There! there! O blessed Lady, protect us!"

"Where?" asked Eustace, scarce able to defend himself from an impression of terror.

"'Tis gone—yet methought I saw it again.—There! look yonder, Sir Knight— something white fluttering behind that column!"

Gaston crossed himself, and turned pale; but Eustace had settled his nerves. "A truce with these vain follies, Master Seneschal," said he, sternly. "Those who know Le Borgne Basque cannot believe his fears, either of saints or demons, to be other than assumed."

No ghost could have startled the Seneschal of the Chateau Norbelle as much as this sobriquet. He fell back, and subsided into complete silence, as he meditated whether it were best to confess the plot, and throw himself upon Sir Eustace's mercy, or whether he could hope that this was merely a chance recognition. He inclined to the latter belief when he observed that the Knight was at fault respecting the secret passage, searching in vain through every part of the vault, and twice passing over the very spot. The third time, however, it so chanced that his spur rung against something of metal, and he called for Gaston to hold his torch lower. The light fell not only upon an iron ring, but upon a guard which evidently covered a key-hole.

Sanchez, after in vain professing great amazement, and perfect ignorance of any such entrance, gave up his bunch of keys, protesting that there was nothing there which could unlock the mysterious door: but the Knight had another method.

"Look you, Master Sanchez," said he, "it may be, as you say, that this door hath not been unclosed for hundreds of years, notwithstanding I see traces in the dust as if it had been raised of late. I shall, however, sleep more securely if convinced that it is an impossibility to lift it. Go, therefore, Gaston, and call half a dozen of the men, to bring each of them the heaviest stone they can find from that heap I saw prepared for a mangonel in the court-yard."

"Oh, excellent!" exclaimed Gaston, "and yet, Sir Eustace—"

There he stopped, but it was evident that he was reluctant to leave his master alone with this villain. Eustace replied by drawing his good sword, and giving him a fearless smile, as he planted his foot upon the trap-door; and fixing his gaze upon Le Borgne Basque, made him feel that this was no moment for treachery.

Gaston sped fast out of the dungeon, and, in brief space, made his appearance at the head of the men-at-arms, some bearing torches, others labouring under the weight of the huge stones, which, as he rightly thought, they were far more inclined to heave at Sir Eustace's head than to place in the spot he pointed out. They were, however, compelled to obey, and, with unwilling hands, built up such a pile upon the secret door, that it could not be lifted from beneath without gigantic strength, and a noise which would re-echo through the Castle. This done, Sir Eustace watched them all out of the vault himself, closed the door, locked it, and announced to the Seneschal his intention of relieving him for the future from the care of the keys. Still watching him closely, he ascended to the hall, and gave the signal for the supper, which shortly made its appearance.

Thibault Sanchez, who laid claim to some share of gentle blood, was permitted to enjoy the place of honour together with Sir Eustace and d'Aubricour—the rather that it gave them a better opportunity of keeping their eye upon him.

There was an evident attempt, on the part of the garrison, to engage their new comrades in a carouse in honour of their arrival, but this was brought to an abrupt conclusion by Sir Eustace, who, in a tone which admitted no reply, ordered the wine flasks to the buttery, and the men, some to their posts and others to their beds. Ingram walked off, muttering his discontent; and great was the ill-will excited amongst, not only the original garrison, but the new-comers from Bordeaux, who, from their lairs of straw, lamented the day when they took service with so severe and rigid a Knight, and compared his discipline with that of his brother, Sir Reginald, who, strict as he might be, never grudged a poor man-at-arms a little merriment. "But as to this Knight, one might as well serve a Cistercian monk!"

As to Le Borgne Basque, he betook himself to the buttery; and there, in an undertone of great terror, began to mutter to his friend and ally, Tristan de la Fleche, "It is all over with us! He is a wizard! Sir Leonard Ashton was right—oaf as he was; I never believed him before; but what, save enchantment, could have enabled him to recognize me under this disguise, or how could he have gone straight to yonder door?"

"Think you not that he had some warning?" asked Tristan.

"Impossible, save from Clarenham, or from Ashton himself; and, dolt as he is, I trow he has sense enough to keep his own counsel. He has not forgotten the day

72

when he saw this dainty young sprig rise up in his golden spurs before his eyes. I know how it is! It is with him as it was with the Lord of Corasse!"

"How was that, Thibault?"

"Why, you must know that Raymond de Corasse had helped himself to the tithes of a certain Church in Catalonia, whereby the Priest who claimed them said to him, 'Know that I will send thee a champion that thou wilt be more afraid of than thou hast hitherto been of me.' Three months after, each night, in the Castle of Corasse, began such turmoil as never was known; raps at every door, and especially that of the Knight—as if all the goblins in fairy-land had been let loose. The Knight lay silent all one night; but the next, when the rioting was renewed as loud as ever, he leapt out of his bed, and bawled out, 'Who is it at this hour thus knocks at my chamber door?' He was answered, 'It is I.' 'And who sends thee hither?' asked the Knight. 'The Clerk of Catalonia, whom thou hast much wronged. I will never leave thee quiet until thou hast rendered him a just account.' 'What art thou called,' said the Knight, 'who art so good a messenger?' 'Orthon is my name.' But it fell out otherwise from the Clerk's intentions, for Orthon had taken a liking to the Knight, and promised to serve him rather than the Clerk—engaging never to disturb the Castle—for, indeed, he had no power to do ill to any. Often did he come to the Knight's bed by night, and pull the pillow from under his head—"

"What was he like?" asked Tristan.

"The Lord de Corasse could not tell; he only heard him—he never saw aught; for Orthon only came by night, and, having wakened him, would begin by saying, 'he was come from England, Hungary, or elsewhere,' and telling all the news of the place."

"And what think you was he?"

"That was what our Lord, the Count de Foix, would fain have known, when he had much marveled at the tidings that were brought him by the Lord de Corasse, and had heard of the strange messenger who brought them. He entreated the Knight to desire Orthon to show himself in his own proper form—and then, having seen, to describe him.

"So at night, when Orthon came again, and plucked away the pillow, the Knight asked him from whence he came? 'From Prague, in Bohemia,' answered Orthon. 'How far is it?'—'Sixty days' journey.' 'Hast thou returned thence in so short a time?'—'I travel as fast as the wind, or faster.' 'What! hast thou got wings?'—'Oh, no.' 'How, then, canst thou fly so fast?'—'That is no business of yours!' 'No,' said the Knight—'I should like exceedingly to see what form thou hast.'—'That concerns you not,' replied Orthon; 'be satisfied that you hear me.' 'I should love thee better had I seen thee,' said the Knight,—whereupon Orthon promised that the first thing he should see to-morrow, on quitting his bed, should be no other than himself."

"Ha! then, I wager that he saw one of the black cats that played round young Ashton's bed."

"Nay, the Knight's lady would not rise all day lest she should see Orthon; but the Knight, leaping up in the morning, looked about, but could see nothing unusual. At night, when Orthon came, he reproached him for not having shown himself, as he had promised. 'I have,' replied Orthon. 'I say No,' said the Knight. 'What! you saw nothing when you leapt out of bed?'—'Yes,' said the Lord de Corasse, after having considered awhile, 'I saw two straws, which were turning and playing together on the floor.' 'That was myself,' said Orthon.

"The Knight now desired importunately that Orthon would show himself in his own true shape. Orthon told him that it might lead to his being forced to quit his service—but he persisted, and Orthon promised to show himself when first the Knight should leave his chamber in the morning. Therefore, as soon as he was dressed, the Knight went to a window overlooking the court, and there he beheld nothing but a large lean sow, so poor, that she seemed nothing but skin and bone, with long hanging ears, all spotted, and a thin sharp-pointed snout. The Lord de Corasse called to his servants to set the dogs on the ill-favoured creature, and kill it; but, as the kennel was opened, the sow vanished away, and was never seen afterwards. Then the Lord de Corasse returned pensive to his chamber, fearing that the sow had indeed been Orthon!—and truly Orthon never returned more to his bed-side. Within a year, the Knight was dead!"

"Is it true, think you, Sanchez?"

"True! why, man, I have seen the Chateau de Corasse, seven leagues from Orthes!"

"And what think you was Orthon?"

"It is not for me to say; but, you see, there are some who stand fair in men's eyes, who have strange means of gaining intelligence! It will be a merit to weigh down a score of rifled Priests, if we can but circumvent a wizard such as this!"

"But he has brought his books! I saw that broad-faced Englishman carry up a whole pile of them," cried Tristan, turning pale. "With his books he will be enough to conjure us all into apes!"

"Now or never," said Sanchez, encouragingly.

"When all is still, I will go round and waken our comrades, while you creep forth by the hole beneath the bartizan, and warn Clisson that the secret passage is nought, but that when he sees a light in old Montfort's turret—"

Tristan suddenly trod on his foot, as a sign of silence, as a step descended the stairs, and Sir Eustace stood before them.

"You appear to be agreeably employed, gentlemen," said he, glancing at the stoup of wine which was before them; "but my orders are as precise as Norman William's. No lights in this Castle, save my own, after eight o'clock. To your beds, gentlemen, and a good night to you!" He was still fully armed, so that it was unsafe to attack him. And he saw them up the spiral stairs that led from the hall, and watched them enter the narrow dens that served them as sleeping rooms, where many a curse was uttered on the watchfulness of the wizard Knight. At the turn of midnight, Le Borgne Basque crept forth, in some hope that there might be an opportunity of fulfilling his designs, and earning the reward promised him both by Clarenham and the French. But he had not descended far before a red gleam of torchlight was seen on the dark stairs, and, ere he could retreat, the black head and dark eyes of Gaston appeared, glancing with mischievous amusement, as he said, in his gay voice, "You are on the alert, my old comrade. You have not forgotten your former habits when in command here. But Sir Eustace intrusts the care of changing the guard to none but me; so I will not trouble you to disturb yourself another night." And the baffled miscreant retreated.

In this manner passed day after day, in a tacit yet perpetual war between the Knight and the garrison. Not a step could be taken, scarce a word spoken, without some instant reminder that either Sir Eustace or Gaston was on the watch. On the borders of the enemy's country, there was so much reason for vigilance, that the garrison could not reasonably complain of the services required of them; the perpetual watch, and numerous guards; the occupations which Knight and Squire seemed never weary of devising for the purpose of keeping them separate, and their instant prohibition of any attempt at the riotous festivity which was their only consolation for the want of active exercises. They grew heartily weary, and fiercely impatient of restraint, and though the firm, calm, steady strictness of the Knight was far preferable to the rude familiarity and furious passions of many a Castellane, there were many of the men-at-arms who, though not actually engaged in the conspiracy, were impatient of what they called his haughtiness and rigidity. These men were mercenaries from different parts of France, accustomed to a lawless life, and caring little or nothing whatever whether it were beneath the standard of King Charles or King Edward that they acquired pay and plunder. The Englishmen were, of course, devoted to their King and Prince, and though at times unruly, were completely to be depended upon. Yet, while owning Sir Eustace to be a brave, gallant, and kind-hearted Knight, there were times when even they felt a shudder of dread and almost of hatred pass over them, when tales were told of the supernatural powers he was supposed to possess; when Leonard Ashton's adventure with the cats was narrated, or the story of his sudden arrival at Lynwood Keep on the night before the lady's funeral. His own immediate attendants might repel the charge with honest indignation, but many a stout warrior slunk off in terror to bed from the sight of Sir Eustace, turning the pages of one of his heavy books by the light of the hall fire, and saw in each poor bat that flitted about within the damp depths of the vaulted chambers the familiar spirit which brought him exact intelligence of all that passed at Bordeaux, at Paris, or in London. Nay, if he only turned his eyes on the ground, he was thought to be looking for the twisting straws.

CHAPTER XIII

There was a village at some distance from the Chateau Norbelle, the inhabitants of which were required to furnish it with provisions. The Castellane, by paying just prices, and preventing his men from treating the peasants in the cruel and exacting manner to which they were accustomed, had gained their good-will. Prompt intelligence of the proceedings of the French army was always brought to him, and he was thus informed that a large treasure was on its way from Bayonne to Carcasonne, being the subsidy promised by Enrique, King of Castile, to his allies, Bertrand du Guesclin and Oliver de Clisson.

It became the duty of the English to intercept these supplies, and Eustace knew that he should incur censure should he allow the occasion to pass. But how divide his garrison? Which of the men-at-arms could be relied on? After consultation with d'Aubricour, it was determined that he himself should remain with John Ingram and a sufficient number of English to keep the traitors in check, while Gaston went forth in command of the party, who were certain to fight with a good will where spoil was the object. They would be absent at least two nights, since the pass of the Pyrenees, where they intended to lie in ambush, was at a considerable distance, nor was the time of the arrival of the convoy absolutely certain.

The expedition proved completely successful, and on the morning of the third day the rising sun beheld Gaston d'Aubricour riding triumphantly at the head of his little band, in the midst of which was a long line of heavily-laden baggage mules. The towers of Chateau Norbelle appeared in his view, when suddenly with a cry of amazement he perceived that the pennon of St. George and the banner of Lynwood were both absent from the Keep. He could scarcely believe his eyes, but forcing his horse onward with furious impetuosity to obtain a nearer view, he discovered that it was indeed true.

"The miscreants!" he shouted. "Oh, my Knight, my Knight!" and turning to the men who followed him, he exclaimed, "There is yet hope! Will you see our trust betrayed, our noble Knight foully murdered and delivered to his enemies, or will ye strike a bold stroke in his defence? He who is not dead to honour, follow me!"

There was a postern, of which Eustace had given Gaston the key, on his departure, and thither the faithful Squire hastened, without looking back to see whether he was followed by many or few—in fact, rather ready to die with Sir Eustace than hoping to rescue him. The ten Englishmen and some eight Frenchmen, infected by the desperation of his manner, followed him closely as he rushed up the slope, dashed through the moat, and in another moment, opening the door, burst into the court. There stood a party of the garrison, upon whom he rushed with a shout of "Death, death to the traitor!" Gaston's arm did the work of three, as he hewed down the villains, who, surprised and discomfited, made feeble resistance. Who they were, or how many, he saw not, he cared not, but struck right and left, till the piteous cries for mercy, in familiar tones, made some impression, and he paused, as did his companions, while, in a tone of rage and anguish, he demanded, "Where is Sir Eustace?"

"Ah! Master d'Aubricour, 'twas not me, 'twas the traitor, Sanchez—'twas Tristan," was the answer. "Oh, mercy, for our blessed Lady's sake!"

"No mercy, dogs! till ye have shown me Sir Eustace in life and limb."

"Alas! alas! Master d'Aubricour!" This cry arose from some of the English; and Gaston, springing towards the bartizan, beheld the senseless form of his beloved Knight lying stretched in a pool of his own blood! Pouring out lamentations in the passionate terms of the South, tearing his hair at having been beguiled into leaving the Castle, and vowing the most desperate vengeance against Clarenham and his accomplices, he lifted his master from the ground, and, as he did so, he fancied he felt a slight movement of the chest, and a faint moan fell upon his ear.

76

What recked Gaston that the Castle was but half taken, that enemies were around on every side? He saw only, heard only, thought only, of Sir Eustace! What was life or death, prosperity or adversity, save as shared with him! He lifted the Knight in his arms, and, hurrying up the stone steps, placed him on his couch.

"Bring water! bring wine!" he shouted as he crossed the hall. A horse-boy followed with a pitcher of water, and Gaston, unfastening the collar of his doublet, raised his head, held his face towards the air, and deluged it with water, entreating him to look up and speak.

A few long painful gasps, and the eyes were half unclosed, while a scarce audible voice said, "Gaston! is it thou? I deemed it was over!" and then the eyes closed again. Gaston's heart was lightened at having heard that voice once more, even had that word been his last—and answering, "Ay, truly, Sir Knight, all is well so you will but look up," he succeed in pouring a little water into his mouth.

He was interrupted by several of the men-at-arms, who came trooping up to the door, looking anxiously at the wounded Knight, while the foremost said, "Master Gaston, here is gear which must be looked to. Thibault Sanchez and half a dozen more have drawn together in Montfort's tower, and swear they will not come forth till we have promised their lives."

"Give them no such pledge!—Hang without mercy!" cried another voice from behind. "Did not I myself hear the traitorous villains send off Tristan de la Fleche to bear the news to Carcassonne? We shall have the butcher of Bretagne at our throats before another hour is over."

"Cowardly traitor!" cried Gaston. "Wherefore didst thou not cut the throat of the caitiff, and make in to the rescue of the Knight?"

"Why, Master d'Aubricour, the deed was done ere I was well awake, and when it was done, and could not be undone, and we were but four men to a dozen, what could a poor groom do? But you had better look to yourself; for it is true as the legends of the saints, that Tristan is gone to Carcassonne, riding full speed on the Knight's own black charger!"

The news seemed to have greater effect in restoring Eustace than any of Gaston's attentions. He again opened his eyes, and made an effort to raise his head, as he said, almost instinctively, "Secure the gates! Warders, to your posts!"

The men stood amazed; and Eustace, rallying, looked around him, and perceived the state of the case. "Said you they had sent to summon the enemy?" said he.

"Martin said so," replied Gaston, "and I fear it is but too true."

"Not a moment to be lost!" said Eustace. "Give me some wine!" and he spoke in a stronger voice, "How many of you are true to King Edward and to the Prince? All who will not fight to the death in their cause have free leave to quit this Castle; but, first, a message must be sent to Bordeaux."

"True, Sir Eustace, but on whom can we rely?" asked Gaston.

"Alas! I fear my faithful Ingram must be slain," said the Knight, "else this could never have been. Know you aught of him?" he added, looking anxiously at the men.

The answer was a call from one of the men: "Here, John, don't stand there grunting like a hog; the Knight is asking for you, don't you hear?"

A slight scuffle was heard, and in a few seconds the broad figure of Ingram shouldered through the midst of the men-at-arms. He came, almost like a man in a dream, to the middle of the room, and there, suddenly dropping upon his knees, he clasped his hands, exclaiming, "I, John Ingram, hereby solemnly vow to our blessed Lady of Taunton, and St. Joseph of Glastonbury, that never more will I drink sack, or wine or any other sort or kind, spiced or unspiced, on holiday or common day, by day or night. So help me, our blessed Lady and St. Joseph."

"Stand up, John, and let us know if you are in your senses," said Gaston, angrily; "we have no time for fooleries. Let us know whether you have been knave, traitor, or fool; for one or other you must have been, to be standing here sound and safe."

"You are right, Sir Squire," said Ingram, covering his face with his hands. "I would I were ten feet underground ere I had seen this day;" and he groaned aloud.

"You have been deceived by their arts," said Eustace. "That I can well believe; but that you should be a traitor, never, my trusty John!"

"Blessings on you for the word, Sir Eustace!" cried the yeoman, while tears fell down his rough cheeks. "Oh! all the wine in the world may be burnt to the very dregs ere I again let a drop cross my lips! but it was drugged, Sir Eustace, it was drugged—that will I aver to my dying day."

"I believe it," said Eustace; "but we must not wait to hear your tale, John. You must take horse and ride with all speed to Bordeaux. One of you go and prepare a horse—"

"Take Brigliador!" said Gaston; "he is the swiftest. Poor fellow! well that I spared him from our journey amid the mountain passes."

"Then," proceeded Eustace, "bear the news of our case—that we have been betrayed—that Clisson will be on us immediately—that we will do all that man can do to hold out till succour can come, which I pray the Prince to send us."

"Take care to whom he addresses himself," said Gaston. "To some our strait will be welcome news."

"True," said Eustace. "Do thy best to see Sir John Chandos, or, if he be not at the court, prefer thy suit to the Prince himself—to any save the Earl of Pembroke. Or if thou couldst see little Arthur, it might be best of all. Dost understand my orders, John?"

"Ay, Sir," said Ingram, shaking his great head, while the tears still flowed down his cheeks; "but to see you in this case!"

"Think not of that, kind John," said Eustace; "death must come sooner or later, and a sword-cut is the end for a Knight."

"You will not, shall not die, Sir Eustace!" cried Gaston. "Your wounds—"

"I know not, Gaston; but the point is now, not of saving my life, but the Castle. Speed, speed, Ingram! Tell the Prince, if this Castle be taken, it opens the way to Bordeaux itself. Tell him how many brave men it contains, and say to him that I pray him not to deem that Eustace Lynwood hath disgraced his knighthood. Tell Arthur, too, to bear me sometimes in mind, and never forget the line he comes of. Fare thee well, good John!"

78

"Let me but hear that I have your forgiveness, Sir Knight."

"You have it, as freely as I hope for mercy. One thing more: should you see Leonard Ashton, let him know that I bear him no ill-will, and pray him not to leave the fair fame of his old comrade foully stained. Farewell: here is my hand—do not take it as scorn that it is my left—my right I cannot move—"

The yeoman still stood in a sort of trance, gazing at him, as if unable to tear himself away.

"See him off, Gaston," said the Knight; "then have the walls properly manned—all is in your hands."

Gaston obeyed, hurrying him to the gate, and giving him more hope of Sir Eustace's recovery than he felt; for he knew that nothing but the prospect of saving him was likely to inspire the yeoman with either speed or pertinacity enough to be of use. He fondly patted Brigliador, who turned his neck in amaze at finding it was not his master who mounted him, and having watched them for a moment, he turned to look round the court, which was empty, save for the bodies of those whom he had slain in his furious onset. He next repaired to the hall, where he found the greater part of the men loitering about and exchanging different reports of strange events which had taken place:—"He can't be a wizard, for certain," said one, "or he never would be in this case, unless his bargain was up."

"It were shame not to stand by him now in the face of the enemy," said another. "How bold he spoke, weak and wounded as he was!"

"He is of the old English stock," said a third,—"a brave, stout-hearted young Knight."

"Well spoken, old Simon Silverlocks," said Gaston, entering. "I doubt where you would find another such within the wide realm of France."

"He is brave enough, that no man doubts," answered Simon, "but somewhat of the strictest, especially considering his years. Sir Reginald was nothing to him."

"Was it not time to be strict when there was such a nest of treachery within the Castle?" said Gaston. "We knew that murderous miscreant of a Basque, and had we not kept well on our guard against him, you, Master Simon, would long since have been hanging as high from Montfort's tower as I trust soon to see him."

"But how knew you him, Master d'Aubricour? that is the question," said old Simon with a very solemn face of awe.

"How? why by means of somewhat sharper eyes than you seem to possess. I have no time to bandy words—all I come to ask is, will you do the duty of honest men or not? If not, away with you, and I and the Knight will abide here till it pleases Messire Oliver, the butcher, to practice his trade on us. I remember, if some of the Lances of Lynwood do not, a certain camp at Valladolid, when some of us might have been ill off had he not stood by our beds of sickness; nor will I easily desert that pennon which was so gallantly made a banner."

These were remembrances to stir the hearts of the ancient Lances of Lynwood, and there was a cry among them of, "We will never turn our backs on it! Lynwood for ever!"

"Right, mine old comrades. Our walls are strong; our hearts are stronger; three days, and aid must come from Bordeaux. The traitors are captives, and we know to whom to trust; for ye, of English birth, and ye, my countrymen, who made in so boldly to the rescue, ye will not fail at this pinch, and see a brave and noble Knight yielded to a pack of cowardly murderers."

"Never! never! We will stand by him to the last drop of our blood," they replied; for the sight of the brave wounded Knight, as well as the example of Gaston's earnestness and devotion, had had a powerful effect, and they unanimously joined the Squire in a solemn pledge to defend both Castle and Knight to the last extremity.

"Then up with the good old banner!" said Gaston, "and let us give Messire Oliver such a reception as he will be little prepared for." He then gave some hasty directions, appointed old Silverlocks, a skilled and tried warrior, to take the place of Seneschal for the time, and to superintend the arrangements; and sending two men to guard the entrance of Montfort's tower, where Sanchez and his accomplices had shut themselves up, he returned to the Castellane's chamber.

Never was there an apartment more desolate. Chateau Norbelle was built more to be defended than to be inhabited, and the rooms were rather so much inclosed space than places intended for comfort. The walls were of unhewn stone, and, as well as the roof, thickly tapestried with cobwebs,—the narrow loophole which admitted light was unglazed,—and there was nothing in the whole chamber that could be called furniture, save the two rude pallets which served the Knight and Squire for beds, and a chest which had been forced open and rifled by the mutineers. They had carried off Eustace's beloved books, to burn them in the court as instruments of sorcery, and a few garments it had likewise contained lay scattered about the room. Gaston hastened to the side of his beloved Knight, almost dreading, from his silence and stillness, to find him expiring. But he was only faint and exhausted, and when Gaston raised him, and began to examine his wounds, he looked up, saying, "Thanks, thanks, kind Gaston! but waste not your time here. The Castle! the Castle!"

"What care I for the Castle compared to your life!" said Gaston.

"For my honour and your own," said Eustace, fixing his eyes on his Squire's face. "Gaston, I fear you," he added, stretching out his hand and grasping that of d'Aubricour; "if you survive, you will forget the duty you owe the King, for the purpose of avenging me upon Clarenham. If ever you have loved me, Gaston, give me your solemn promise that this shall not be."

"It was the purpose for which I should have lived," said Gaston.

"You resign it?" said Eustace, still retaining his hold of his hand. "You touch not one of my wounds till you have given me your oath."

"I swear it, then," said Gaston, "since you will ever have your own way, and I do it the rather that Messire Oliver de Clisson will probably save me the pain of keeping the pledge."

"You have taken all measures for defence?"

"Yes. The men-at-arms, such as are left, may be trusted, and have all taken an oath to stand by us, which I do not think they will readily break. The rest either made off with the baggage-mules, or were slain when we broke in to your rescue, or are shut up with Le Borgne Basque in Montfort's tower. I have sent the men to their posts, put them under Silverlock's orders, and told him to come to me for directions."

Eustace at last resigned himself into the Squire's hands. A broken arm, a ghastly-looking cut on the head, and a deep thrust with a poniard in the breast, seemed the most serious of the injuries he had received; but there were numerous lesser gashes and stabs which had occasioned a great effusion of blood, and he had been considerably bruised by his fall.

Gaston could attempt nothing but applying some ointment, sold by a Jew at Bordeaux as an infallible cure for all wounds and bruises; and, having done all he could for the comfort of his patient, quitted him to attend to the defence of the Castle.

His first visit was to Montfort's tower, one of the four flanking the main body of the Castle.

"Well, Master Thibault Sanchez, or, if you like it better, Le Borgne Basque," cried he, "thank you for saving us some trouble. You have found yourself a convenient prison there, and I hope you are at your ease."

"We shall see how you are at your ease, Master Gaston le Maure," retorted Sanchez from the depths of the tower, "when another Borgne shall make his appearance, and string you up as a traitor to King Charles, your liege lord."

"Le Borgne Basque talking of traitors and such gear!" returned Gaston; "but he will tell a different tale when the succours come from the Prince."

"Ha! ha!" laughed Thibault, "a little bird whispered in mine ear that you may look long for succour from Bordeaux."

This was, in a great measure, Gaston's own conviction; but he only replied the more vehemently that it could not fail, since neither Knights nor Castles were so lightly parted with, and that he trusted soon to have the satisfaction of seeing the inhabitants of the tower receive the reward of their treachery.

Thus they parted—Thibault, perfectly well satisfied to remain where he was, since he had little doubt that Oliver de Clisson's speedy arrival would set him at liberty, and turn the tables upon Gaston; and Gaston, glad that, since he could not at present have the satisfaction of hanging him, he was in a place where he could do no mischief, and whence he could not escape.

Now the warder on the watch-tower blew a blast, and every eye was turned towards the eastern part of the country, where, in the direction of Carcassonne, was to be seen a thick cloud of dust, from which, in due time, were visible the flashes of armour, and the points of weapons. Gaston, having given his orders, and quickened the activity of each man in his small garrison, hurried down to bear the tidings to Sir Eustace, and to array himself in his own brightest helmet and gayest surcoat.

Ascending again to the battlements, he could see the enemy approaching, could distinguish the banner of Clisson, and count the long array of men-at-arms and crossbow-men as they pursued their way through the bright green landscape, now half hidden by a rising ground, now slowly winding from its summit.

At last they came to the foot of the slope. Gaston had already marked the start

81

and pause, which showed when they first recognized the English standard; and there was another stop, while they ranged themselves in order, and, after a moment's interval, a man-at-arms rode forward towards the postern door, looked earnestly at it, and called "Sanchez!"

"Shoot him dead!" said Gaston to an English crossbow-man who stood beside him; "it is the villain Tristan, on poor Ferragus."

The arblast twanged, and Tristan fell, while poor Ferragus, after starting violently, trotted round to the well-known gate, and stood there neighing. "Poor fellow!" said Gaston, "art calling Brigliador? I would I knew he had sped well."

The French, dismayed by the reception of their guide, held back; but presently a pursuivant came forward from their ranks, and, after his trumpet had been sounded, summoned, in the name of the good Knight, Messire Oliver de Clisson, the garrison of Chateau Norbelle to surrender it into his hands, as thereto commissioned by his grace, Charles, King of France.

The garrison replied by another trumpet, and Gaston, standing forth upon the battlements, over the gateway, demanded to speak with Sir Oliver de Clisson, and to have safe-conduct to and from the open space at the foot of the slope. This being granted, the drawbridge was lowered, and the portcullis raised. Ferragus entered, and went straight to his own stall; and Gaston d'Aubricour came forth in complete armour, and was conducted by the pursuivant to the leader of the troop. Sir Oliver de Clisson, as he sat on horseback with the visor of his helmet raised, had little or nothing of the appearance of the courteous Knight of the period. His features were not, perhaps, originally as harsh and ill-formed as those of his compeer, Bertrand du Guesclin, but there was a want of the frank open expression and courteous demeanour which so well suited the high chivalrous temper of the great Constable of France. They were dark and stern, and the loss of an eye, which had been put out by an arrow, rendered him still more hard-favoured. He was, in fact, a man soured by early injuries—his father had been treacherously put to death by King John of France, when Duke of Normandy, and his brother had been murdered by an Englishman—his native Brittany was torn by dissensions and divisions—and his youth had been passed in bloodshed and violence. He had now attained the deserved fame of being the second Knight in France, honourable and loyal as regarded his King, but harsh, rigid, cruel, of an unlovable temper, which made him in after years a mark for plots and conspiracies; and the vindictive temper of the Celtic race leading him to avenge the death of his brother upon every Englishman who fell into his hands.

"So, Sir Squire!" exclaimed he, in his harsh voice, "what excuse do you come to make for slaying my messenger ere he had time to deliver his charge?"

"I own him as no messenger," returned Gaston. "He was a renegade traitor from our own Castle, seeking his accomplice in villainy!"

"Well, speak on," said Oliver, to whom the death of a man-at-arms was a matter of slight importance. "Art thou come to deliver up the Castle to its rightful lord?"

"No, Messire Oliver," replied Gaston. "I come to bring the reply of the Castellane, Sir Eustace Lynwood, that he will hold out the Castle to the last extremity against all and each of your attacks."

"Sir Eustace Lynwood? What means this, Master Squire? Yonder knave declared he was dead!"

"Hear me, Sir Oliver de Clisson," said Gaston. "Sir Eustace Lynwood hath a pair of mortal foes at the Prince's court, who prevailed on a part of the garrison to yield him into your hands. In my absence, they in part succeeded. By the negligence of a drunken groom they were enabled to fall upon him in his sleep, and, as they deemed, had murdered him. I, returning with the rest of the garrison, was enabled to rescue him, and deliver the Castle, where he now lies—alive, indeed, but desperately wounded. Now, I call upon you, Sir Oliver, to judge, whether it be the part of a true and honourable Knight to become partner of such miscreants, and to take advantage of so foul a web of treachery?"

"This may be a fine tale for the ears of younger knights-errant, Sir Squire," was the reply of Clisson. "For my part though I am no lover of treason, I may not let the King's service be stayed by scruples. For yourself, Sir Squire, I make you a fair offer. You are, by your tongue and countenance, a Gascon—a liegeman born of King Charles of France. To you, and to every other man of French birth, I offer to enter his service, or to depart whither it may please you, with arms and baggage, so you will place the Castle in our hands—and leave us to work our will of the island dogs it contains!"

"Thanks, Sir Oliver, for such a boon as I would not vouchsafe to stoop to pick up, were it thrown at my feet!"

"Well and good, Sir Squire," said Clisson, rather pleased at the bold reply. "We understand each other. Fare thee well."

And Gaston walked back to the Castle, muttering to himself, "Had it been but the will of the Saints to have sent Du Guesclin hither, then would Sir Eustace have been as safe and free as in Lynwood Keep itself! But what matters it? If he dies of his wounds, what good would my life do me, save to avenge him—and from that he has debarred me. So, grim Oliver, do thy worst!—Ha!" as he entered the Castle—"down portcullis—up drawbridge! Archers, bend your bows! Martin, stones for the mangonel!"

Nor was the assault long delayed. Clisson's men only waited to secure their horses and prepare their ladders, and the attack was made on every side.

It was well and manfully resisted. Bravely did the little garrison struggle with the numbers that poured against them on every side, and the day wore away in the desperate conflict.

Sir Eustace heard the loud cries of "Montjoie St. Denis! Clisson!" on the one side, and the "St. George for Merry England! A Lynwood!" with which his own party replied; he heard the thundering of heavy stones, the rush of combatants, the cries of victory or defeat. Sometimes his whole being seemed in the fight; he clenched his teeth, he shouted his war-cry, tried to raise himself and lift his powerless arm; then returned again to the consciousness of his condition, clasped either the rosary or the crucifix, and turned his soul to fervent prayer; then, again, the strange wild cries without confounded themselves into one maddening noise on his feverish ear, or, in the confusion of his weakened faculties, he would, as it were, believe himself to be his brother dying on the field of Navaretta, and scarce be able to rouse himself to a feeling of his own identity.

So passed the day—and twilight was fast deepening into night, when the cries, a short time since more furious than ever, and nearer and more exulting on the part of the French, at length subsided, and finally died away; the trampling steps of the men-at-arms could be heard in the hall below, and Gaston himself came up with hasty step, undid his helmet, and, wiping his brow, threw himself on the ground with his back against the chest, saying, "Well, we have done our devoir, at any rate! Poor Brigliador! I am glad he has a kind master in Ingram!"

"Have they won the court?" asked Eustace. "I thought I heard their shouts within it."

"Ay! Even so. How could we guard such an extent of wall with barely five and twenty men? Old Silverlocks and Jaques de l'Eure are slain Martin badly wounded, and we all forced back into the inner court, after doing all it was in a man to do."

"I heard your voice, bold and cheerful as ever, above the tumult," said Eustace. "But the inner court is fit for a long defence—that staircase parapet, where so few can attack at once."

"Ay," said Gaston, "it was that and the darkness that stopped them. There I can detain them long enough to give the chance of the succours, so those knaves below do not fail in spirit—and they know well enough what chance they have from yon grim-visaged Breton! But as to those succours, I no more expect them than I do to see the Prince at their head! A hundred to one that he never hears of our need, or, if he should, that Pembroke and Clarenham do not delay the troops till too late."

"And there will be the loss of the most important castle, and the most faithful and kindest heart!" said Eustace. "But go, Gaston—food and rest you must need after this long day's fight—and the defences must be looked to, and the men cheered!"

"Yes," said Gaston, slowly rising, and bending over the Knight; "but is there nought I can do for you, Sir Eustace?"

"Nought, save to replenish my cup of water. It is well for me that the enemy have not cut us off from the Castle well."

Gaston's supper did not occupy him long. He was soon again in Eustace's room, talking over his plan of defence for the next day; but with little, if any, hope that it would be other than his last struggle. At last, wearied out with the exertions of that day and the preceding, he listened to Eustace's persuasions, and, removing the more cumbrous portions of his armour, threw himself on his bed, and, in a moment, his regular breathings announced that he was sound asleep.

It was in the pale early light of dawn that he awoke, and, starting up while still half asleep, exclaimed, "Sir Eustace, are you there? I should have relieved guard long since!" Then, as he recalled his situation, "I had forgot! How is it with you, Sir Eustace? Have you slept?"

"No," said Eustace. "I have not lost an hour of this last night I shall ever see. It will soon be over now—the sun is already reddening the sky; and so, Gaston, ends our long true-hearted affection. Little did I think it would bring thee to thy death in the prime of they strength and manhood!" and he looked mournfully on the lofty stature and vigorous form of the Squire, as he stood over him.

"For that, Sir Eustace, there is little cause to grieve. I have been a wanderer, friendless and homeless, throughout my life; and save for yourself, and, perhaps, poor little Arthur's kind heart, where is one who would cast a second thought on me, beyond, perhaps, saying, 'He was a brave and faithful Squire!' But little, little did I think, when I saw your spurs so nobly won, that this was to be the end of it —that you were to die, defamed and reviled, in an obscure den, and by the foul treachery of—"

"Speak not of that, Gaston," said Eustace. "I have dwelt on it in the long hours of the night, and I have schooled my mind to bear it. Those with whom we shall soon be, know that if I have sinned in many points, yet I am guiltless in that whereof they accuse me—and, for the rest, there are, at least, two who will think no shame of Eustace Lynwood. And now, if there is yet time, Gaston, since no Priest is at hand, I would pray thee to do me the last favour of hearing the confession of my sins."

And Gaston kneeling down, the Knight and Squire, according to the custom of warriors in extremity, confessed to each other, with the crucifix raised between them. Eustace then, with his weak and failing voice, repeated several prayers and psalms appropriate to the occasion, in which Gaston joined with hearty devotion. By this time, a slight stir was heard within the Castle; and Gaston, rising from his knees, went to the loophole, which commanded a view of the court, where the French had taken up their quarters for the night in some of the outbuildings— and the lion rampant of Clisson was waving in triumph on the gateway tower.

"All silent there," said he; "but I must go to rouse our knaves in time to meet the first onset." And, as he clasped on his armour, he continued, "All that is in the power of man will we do! Rest assured, Sir Eustace, they reach you not save through my body; and let your prayers be with me. One embrace, Sir Eustace, and we meet no more—"

"In this world." Eustace concluded the sentence, as Gaston hung over him, and his tears dropped on his face. "Farewell, most faithful and most true-hearted! Go, I command thee! Think not on me—think on thy duty—and good angels will be around us both. Farewell, farewell."

Gaston, for the first time in his life, felt himself unable to speak. He crossed the room with slow and lingering step; then, with a great effort, dashed out at the door, closing his visor as he did so, and, after a short interval, during which he seemed to have stopped on the stairs, Eustace could hear his gay bold tones, calling, "Up! up! my merry men, all! Let not the French dogs find the wolf asleep in his den. They will find our inner bartizan a hard stone for their teeth—and it will be our own fault, if they crack it before the coming of our brave comrades from Bordeaux!"

85

CHAPTER XIV

The open space beyond the walls of Bordeaux presented a bright and lively scene. It was here that the pages of the Black Prince were wont to exercise those sports and pastimes for which the court of the palace scarce offered sufficient space, or which were too noisy for the neighbourhood of the ladies, and of the invalid Prince.

Of noble and often of princely birth were all who entered that school of chivalry, and, for the most part, the fine open countenances, noble bearing, and well-made figures of the boys, testified their high descent, as completely as the armorial bearings embroidered on the back and front of their short kirtles. Many different provinces had sent their noblest to be there trained in the service of the bravest Knights and Princes. There, besides the brown-haired, fair-skinned English boy, was the quick fiery Welsh child, who owned an especial allegiance to the Prince; the broad blue-eyed Fleming, whose parents rejoiced in the fame of the son of Philippa of Hainault; the pert, lively Gascon, and the swarthy Navarrese mountaineer—all brought together in close and ever-changing contrast of countenance, habits, and character.

Of all the merry groups scattered through that wide green space, the most interesting was one formed by three boys, who stood beneath a tree, a little from the rest. The two eldest might be from ten to eleven years old, the third two or three years younger, and his delicate features, fair pale complexion, and slender limbs, made him appear too weak and childish for such active sports as the rest were engaged in, but that the lordly glance of his clear blue eye, his firm tread, and the noble carriage of his shapely head, had in them something of command, which attracted notice even before the exceeding beauty of his perfectly moulded face, and long waving curls of golden hair.

So like him, that they might have passed for brothers, was one of the elder boys, who stood near—there was the same high white brow, proud lip, regular features, and bright eye; but the complexion, though naturally fair, was tanned to a healthy brown where exposed to the sun; the frame was far stronger and more robust; and the glance of the eye had more in it of pride and impatience, than of calm command so remarkable in the little one. The three boys were standing in consultation over an arrow which they had just discovered, stuck deep in the ground.

"'Tis my arrow, that I shot over the mark on Monday," said the elder.

"Nay, Harry," said the younger boy, "that cannot be; for remember Thomas Holland said your arrow would frighten the good nuns of St. Ursula in their garden."

"It must be mine," persisted Harry—"for none of you all can shoot as far."

"Yes, English Arthur can," said the little boy. "He shot a whole cloth-yard beyond you the day—"

"Well, never mind, Edward," said Harry, sharply—"who cares for arrows?— weapons for clowns, and not for Princes!"

"Nay, not so, Lord Harry," interrupted the third boy: "I have heard my uncle say, many a time, that England's archery is half her strength—and how it was our archers at the battle of Crecy—"

"I know all that—how the men of Genoa had wet bow-strings, and ours dry ones," said Henry; "but they were peasants, after all!"

"Ay; but a King of England should know how to praise and value his good yeomen."

Henry turned on his heel, and, saying, "Well, let the arrow be whose it will, I care not for it," walked off.

"Do you know why Harry of Lancaster goes, Arthur?" said Edward, smiling.

"No, my Lord," replied Arthur.

"He cannot bear to hear aught of King of England," was the answer. "If you love me, good Arthur, vex him not with speaking of it."

"Father Cyril would say, he ought to learn content with the rank where he was born," said Arthur.

"Father Cyril, again!" said Prince Edward. "You cannot live a day without speaking of him, and of your uncle."

"I do not speak of them so much now," said Arthur, colouring, "It is only you, Lord Edward, who never make game of me for doing so—though, I trow, I have taught Pierre de Greilly to let my uncle's name alone."

"Truly, you did so," said Edward, laughing, "and he has scarce yet lost his black eye. But I love to hear your tales, Arthur, of that quiet Castle, and the old Blanc Etoile, and your uncle, who taught you to ride. Sit down here on the grass, and tell me more. But what are you staring at so fixedly? At the poor jaded horse, that yonder man-at-arms is urging on so painfully?"

"'Tis—No, it is not—Yes, 'tis Brigliador, and John Ingram himself," cried Arthur. "Oh, my uncle! my uncle!" And, in one moment, he had bounded across the ditch, which fenced in their exercising ground, and had rushed to meet Ingram. "Oh, John!" exclaimed he, breathlessly, "have they done it? Oh, tell me of Uncle Eustace! Is he alive?"

"Master Arthur!" exclaimed Ingram, stopping his wearied horse.

"Oh, tell me, Ingram," reiterated Arthur, "is my uncle safe?"

"He is alive, Master Arthur—that is, he was when I came away, but as sore wounded as ever I saw a Knight. And the butcher of Brittany is upon them by this time! And here I am sent to ask succours—and I know no more whom to address myself, than the cock at the top of Lynwood steeple!"

"But what has chanced, John?—make haste, and tell me."

And John, in his own awkward and confused style, narrated how he had been entrapped by Sanchez, and the consequences of his excess. "But," said he, "I have vowed to our Lady of Taunton, and St. Joseph of Glastonbury, that never again —"

Arthur had covered his face with his hands, and gave way to tears of indignation and grief, as he felt his helplessness. But one hand was kindly withdrawn, and a gentle voice said, "Weep not, Arthur, but come with me, and my father will send relief to the Castle, and save your uncle."

87

"You here, Lord Edward?" exclaimed Arthur, who had not perceived that the Prince had followed him. "Oh yes, thanks, thanks! None but the Prince can save him. Oh, let me see him myself, and that instantly!"

"Then, let us come," said Edward, still holding Arthur's hand.

Arthur set off at such a pace, as to press the little Prince into a breathless trot by his side; but he, too, was all eagerness, and scorned to complain. They proceeded without interruption to the court of the palace. Edward, leading the way, hastened to his mother's apartments. He threw open the door, looked in, and, saying to Arthur, "He must be in the council chamber," cut short an exclamation of Lady Maude Holland, by shutting the door, and running down a long gallery to an ante-chamber, where were several persons waiting for an audience, and two warders, with halberts erect, standing on guard outside a closed door.

"The Prince is in council, my Lord."

Edward drew up his head, and, waving them aside with a gesture that became the heir of England, said, "I take it upon myself." He then opened the door, and, still holding Arthur fast by the hand, led him into the chamber where the Prince of Wales sat in consultation.

There was a pause of amazement as the two boys advanced to the high carved chair on which the Prince was seated—and Edward exclaimed, "Father, save Arthur's uncle!"

"What means this, Edward?" demanded the Prince of Wales, somewhat sternly. "Go to your mother, boy—we cannot hear you now, and—"

"I cannot go, father," replied the child, "till you have promised to save Arthur's uncle! He is wounded!—the traitors have wounded him!—and the French will take the Castle, and he will be slain! And Arthur loves him so much!"

"Come here, Edward," said the Prince, remarking the flushed cheek and tearful eye of his son, "and tell me what this means."

Edward obeyed, but without loosing his hold of his young friend's hand. "The man-at-arms is come, all heat and dust, on the poor drooping, jaded steed—and he said, the Knight would be slain, and the Castle taken, unless you would send him relief. It is Arthur's uncle that he loves so well."

"Arthur's uncle?" repeated the Prince—and, turning his eyes on the suppliant figure, he said, "Arthur Lynwood! Speak, boy."

"Oh, my Lord," said Arthur, commanding his voice with difficulty, "I would only pray you to send succour to my uncle at Chateau Norbelle, and save him from being murdered by Oliver de Clisson."

It was a voice which boded little good to Arthur's suit that now spoke. "If it be Sir Eustace Lynwood, at Chateau Norbelle, of whom the young Prince speaks, he can scarce be in any strait, since the garrison is more than sufficient."

The little page started to his feet, and, regarding the speaker with flashing eyes, exclaimed, "Hearken not to him, my Lord Prince! He is the cause of all the treachery!—he is the ruin and destruction of my uncle;—he has deceived you with his falsehoods!—and now he would be his death!"

"How now, my young cousin!" said Clarenham, in a most irritating tone of indifference—"you forget in what presence you are."

"I do not," replied Arthur, fiercely. "Before the Prince, Fulk Clarenham, I declare you a false traitor!—and, if you dare deny it, there lies my gloves!"

Fulk only replied by a scornful laugh, and, addressing the Prince, said, "May I pray of your Grace not to be over severe with my young malapert relation."

The Captal de Buch spoke: "You do not know what an adversary you have provoked, Fulk! The other day, I met my nephew, little Pierre, with an eye as black as the patch we used to wear in our young days of knight-errantry. 'What wars have you been in, Master Pierre?' I asked. It was English Arthur who had fought with him, for mocking at his talking of nothing but his uncle. But you need not colour, and look so abashed, little Englishman!—I bear no more malice than I hope Pierre does—I only wish I had as bold a champion! I remember thine uncle, if he is the youth to whom the Constable surrendered at Navaretta, and of whom we made so much."

"Too much then, and too little afterwards," said old Sir John Chandos.

"You do not know all, Chandos," said the Prince.

"You do not yourself know all, my Lord," said Arthur, turning eagerly. "Lord de Clarenham has deceived you, and led you to imagine that my uncle wished ill to me, and wanted to gain my lands; whereas it is he himself who wants to have me in his hands to bend me to his will. It is he who has placed traitors in Chateau Norbelle to slay my uncle and deliver him to the enemy; they have already wounded him almost to death"—here Arthur's lips quivered, and he could hardly restrain a burst of tears—"and they have sent for Sir Oliver de Clisson, the butcher. Gaston will hold out as long as they can, but if you will not send succours, my Lord, he will—will be slain; and kind Gaston too;" and Arthur, unable to control himself any longer, covered his face with his hands, and gave way to a silent suppressed agony of sobs and tears.

"Cheer thee, my boy," said the Prince, kindly; "we will see to thine uncle." Then, looking at his nobles, he continued, "It seems that these varlets will allow us no more peace; and since there does in truth appear to be a Knight and Castle in jeopardy, one of you had, perhaps, better go with a small band, and clear up this mystery. If it be as the boy saith, Lynwood hath had foul wrong."

"I care not if I be the one to go, my Lord," said Chandos; "my men are aver kept in readiness, and a night's gallop will do the lazy knaves all the good in the world."

Arthur, brushing off the tears, of which he was much ashamed, looked at the old Knight in transport.

"Thanks, Chandos," said the Prince; "I would commit the matter to none so willingly as to you, though I scarce would have asked it, considering you were not quite so prompt on a late occasion."

"My Lord of Pembroke will allow, however, that I did come in time," said Sir John. "It was his own presumption and foolhardiness that got him into the scrape, and he was none the worse for the lesson he received. But this young fellow seems to have met with this mischance by no fault of his own; and I am willing to see him righted; for he is a good lad as well as a brave, as far as I have known him."

"How came the tidings?" asked the Prince. "Did not one of you boys say somewhat of a man-at-arms?"

"Yes, my Lord," said Arthur; "John Ingram, my uncle's own yeoman, has come upon Brigliador with all speed. I sent him to the guard-room, where he now waits in case you would see him."

"Ay," said old Chandos, "a man would have some assurance that he is not going on a fool's errand. Let us have him here, my Lord."

"Cause him to be summoned," said the Prince to Arthur.

"And at the same time," said Chandos, "send for my Squire, Henry Neville, to the ante-chamber. The men may get on their armour in the meantime."

In a few minutes John Ingram made his appearance, the dust not yet wiped from his armour, his hair hanging is disordered masses over his forehead, and his jaws not completely resting from the mastication of a huge piece of pasty. His tale, though confused, could not be for an instant doubted, as he told of the situation in which he had left Chateau Norbelle and its Castellane, "The best man could wish to live under. Well, he hath forgiven me, and given me his hand upon it."

"Forgiven thee—for what?" said the Prince.

"Ah! my Lord, I may speak of treason, but I am one of the traitors myself! Did not the good Knight leave me in charge to make my rounds constantly in the Castle, while he slept after his long watching? and lo, there comes that wily rascal, the Seneschal, Sanchez, with his "Tis a cold night, friend John; the Knight wakes thee up early; come down to the buttery, and crack a cup of sack in all friendliness!' Down then go I, oaf that I was, thinking that, may be, our Knight was over strict and harsh, and pulled the reins so tight, that a poor man-at-arms must needs get a little diversion now and then—as the proverb says, 'when the cat's away, the mice may play.' But it was drugged, my Lord, else when would one cup of spiced wine have so overcome me that I knew nought till I hear Master d'Aubricour shouting treason in the courtyard like one frantic? But the Knight has forgiven me, and I have sworn to our blessed Lady of Taunton, and St. Joseph of Glastonbury, that not a draught of wine, spiced or unspiced, shall again cross my lips."

"A wholesome vow," said the Prince; "and her is a token to make thee remember it,"—and he placed in the hand of the yeoman a chain of some value. "Go to the guard-room, where you shall be well entertained till such time as we need thee again, as we may, if you have been, as you say, long in Sir Eustace Lynwood's service. But what now? Hast more to say?"

"I would say—so please you, my Lord—that I pray you but to let me ride back to Chateau Norbelle with this honourable Knight, for I owe all service to Sir Eustace, nor could I rest till I know how it fares with him."

"As you will, good fellow," said the Prince; "and you, Chandos, come with me to my chamber—I would speak with you before you depart."

"My Lord," said Arthur, "would you but grant me one boon—to go with Sir John to Chateau Norbelle?"

90

"You too? You would almost make me think you all drawn by witchcraft to this Castle!" But Arthur's eagerness extorted a consent, and he rode off amid Sir John Chandos's troop, boldly enough at first, but by and by so sleepily, that, as night advanced, Sir John ordered him to be placed in front of a trooper, and he soon lost all perception of the rough rapid pace at which they travelled. It was broad day when he was awakened by a halt, and the first thing he heard was, "There is St. George's pennon still safe!"

He sat upright, gazed eagerly forwards, and beheld a tall dark tower rising by the bank of a stream at some distance. "Chateau Norbelle?" he asked.

"Oh, ho! my little page," said Chandos. "You are alive again, are you? Ay, Chateau Norbelle it is—and we are in time it seems! But let us have you on your own steed again. And let us see—if Oliver be there himself, we shall have sharp work. Ay, keep you by the side of the old master leech there—he will be sure to keep out of peril. Now—close in—lances in rest—bows bent. Forward banner!"

Arthur, by no means approving of the companionship assigned him, contrived to wedge in his pony a little in the rear of Sir John's two Squires, as the whole squadron rode down the slope of the hill, and up the ascent on which the Castle stood. Loud cries and shrieks from within began to strike their ears—the clash of arms—all the tumult of attack and defence raging fearfully high and wild.

"Ho, ho! friend Oliver!—we have you in a trap!" said old Chandos, in high glee, as he drew up close without the walls. "Neville, guard the gates!"

He signed to about half his band to remain without, and cut off the retreat of the enemy. The Jew doctor chose his post in their rear, close to the Castle moat—but not so Arthur. Unnoticed and forgotten, he still kept close behind the Squire, who rode alongside of Sir John Chandos, as he crossed the drawbridge. The Castle gate was open, and showed a wild confused mass of struggling men and flashing arms. It was the last, most furious onset, when Clisson, enraged by the long resistance of so weak a garrison, was concentrating his strength in one effort, and, in the excitement of the assault, he had failed to remark that his sentinels had transgressed his orders, and mingled with the crowd, who were striving, by force of numbers, to overwhelm the small troop of defenders of the bartizan.

In rushed Chandos, shouting his war-cry!—In dashed his stout warriors, and loud and fierce pealed forth "St. George! St George!" drowning the now feebler note of "Montjoie, St. Denis!" and fearful were the shrieks of horror and of pain that rose mingled with it. Hemmed in, attacked in front and rear, their retreat cut off, the French looked in vain for escape; some went down beneath the tremendous charge of the English, some cried for mercy, and surrendered as prisoners. Oliver de Clisson himself, seeing that all was lost, swinging round his head his heavy battle-axe, opened for himself a way, and, with a few followers, broke through the men whom Chandos had left outside, and, cutting down a groom who was holding it, captured one of his led horses, on which he rode off at his leisure, confident in his own gigantic strength.

So little resistance had been offered, that Arthur's bold advance had involved him in little danger; he was borne onwards, and only was conscious of a frightful tumult, where all seemed to be striking and crushing together. At last, there was something of a lull; the cries of mercy, and offers to surrender, alone were heard. Arthur found his pony standing still, and himself pressed hither and thither by the crowd, from which he knew not how to escape.

Above these various sounds he heard an opening door—there was a press forward, which carried him with it. The heavy doors, shivered here and there by Clisson's axe, had been thrown wide open; but the crowd closed in—he saw no more. He threw himself from his pony, struggled forwards, and at last, emerging between the arms of two tall men, he beheld Sir John Chandos dismounting from his war-horse, which was held by a grim, bloody, dusty figure in broken armour, whose length of limb, and the crisp, black, curled hair that showed through the shattered helmet, proved that it could be no other than Gaston d'Aubricour.

Arthur darted forwards, his heart upon his lips; but neither Knight nor Squire had eye or ear for him; they were hastily exchanging queries about—he knew not what—they were not of his uncle; and, borne on by his impatience, he hurried past them up the narrow stone stair. More than one corpse—a ghastly sight—lay on the steps, but he hastened on; half a dozen men were standing on the stones at the top, all, like Gaston, dusty and gory, and leaning on their weapons, or on the wall, as if exhausted. They were looking intently at the court, and gave no heed to the boy, as he ran on into the hall. Two men lay there groaning before the fire. Arthur stood and looked round, hesitating whether to ask them for his uncle; but, perceiving the spiral stairs, quickly ascended. Far and far up he wound, till he came to a low-browed arch; he paused, and saw a large vaulted room, through the loop-hole window of which shone a yellow stream of golden sunshine. There was a low bed in one corner, and on it lay a motionless form. On tiptoe, and with a throbbing heart, the boy approached; he saw the face—it was ghastly pale. He stood transfixed—could it be?—yes, it must still be, his own Uncle Eustace.

CHAPTER XV

It was still very early, and the narrow line of sky seen from the turret window was gilded by the bright pale-green light of morning, when Sir Eustace awoke. All around was perfectly still, and he could have believed himself waking merely from a dream of tumult and disturbance, but for his feelings of pain and weakness. At some little distance lay, on a softly-dressed sheepskin, the oriental figure of the Jewish mediciner, and, at the foot of his own bed, the unexpected form of little Arthur reclined, half sitting, half lying, with his head resting on his crossed arms, and his long curls floating over them. All was a riddle to his misty remembrance, clouded by weakness; and, in vague uncertain recollections and conjectures, the time rolled away, till the sounds of awakening and calls of the warders within the Castle betokened that it was occupied by no small number of persons. Still Arthur slept on, and Eustace abstained from the slightest movement that could disturb him, till a step stole quietly to the door, and Gaston's head was seen cautiously and anxiously looking in. Eustace, raising his hand, beckoned him, and made a sign of silence.

"How is with you, Sir Eustace? It must needs be better. I see a light in your eye once more."

"I am another man since yesterday, Gaston; but be careful—see there."

"Little fear of breaking such sleep as that," said Gaston. "'Tis a noble-hearted little fellow, and if matters go better with us henceforth, it will be his work."

"What is become of Clisson?"

"He was riding off headlong when Master Henry Neville last beheld him, gaining thereby a sound rating from old Chandos."

"Sir John Chandos here?"

"Fast asleep in your own carved chair, with his feet on the oaken settle."

"Sir John Chandos!" again exclaimed Eustace.

"Even so. All thanks to the brave young damoiseau who—"

Here Gaston's ardour had the effect of awakening the doctor, who immediately began to grumble at his patient's admitting visitors without permission. By the time he had examined Eustace's wounds and pronounced him to be progressing favourably, the whole Castle was up and awake, and Arthur, against his will, was sent down to attend on Sir John Chandos at breakfast, when scarce satisfied that his uncle could speak to him.

In process of time he came up to announce a visit from Chandos himself, and close on his steps followed the stalwart old warrior. Pausing at the door, he looked around him, struck with the aspect of the dungeon-like apartment, still more rugged in the morning light than in the evening gloom—the bare rough walls, an arrow sticking between the stones immediately above the Knight's head, the want of furniture, the Knight's own mantle and that of Gaston both called into requisition to protect him from the damp chill night air, their bright hues and rich embroidery contrasting with the squalid appearance of all around, as, indeed, did the noble though pale features of the wounded man himself, and the graceful attire and shining hair of the fair young boy who stood over him. But Sir John beheld all with no dissatisfaction.

"Well, my brave young Sir," said he, advancing, "how is it with you this morning? You look cheerily; I trust we shall soon have you on horseback again."

"Thanks to the blessed Saints and to you, Sir John," replied Eustace. "I fear you fared ill last night for,"—and he looked round with a smile—"you see, I occupy the state bed-chamber."

"The better, Sir Eustace," said Chandos. "It does my heart good to see such a chamber as this—none of the tapestry and hangings which our young Knights nowadays fence themselves with, as if they kept out the foe—this is what it is meant for—a stronghold, and not a bower. I'll have my dainty young Master Neville up here, to see how a good Knight should be lodged."

"I fear he would scarce consider it as an example," said Eustace, smiling, "since all our simplicity would not have availed to protect us, but for your coming. We little dreamt to see this morning's light."

"True, but where should I look for a garrison to make such a defence as you and your Squire have done? When I saw the spot, and looked at the numbers, and heard how long you had held out, methought I was returned once more to the good old days of Calais. And here this youth of mine, not yet with his spurs, though I dare say full five years older than you, must needs look sour upon it, because he has to sleep on a settle for one night—and that, too, when he has let Oliver de Clisson slip through his fingers, without so much as a scratch taken or given on either side! It grieves my very soul to think on it! But all has gone to rack and ruin since the Prince has been unable to set the example."

"Is the Prince better in health?"

"Yes—so they say—but his looks tell another tale, and I never expect to see him on horseback again," said the old warrior, with a deep sigh. "But I have to do his bidding here, and have much to ask of you, Sir Eustace; and I do it the more willingly, that I rejoice to see a brave man righted."

"Has the Prince, then, commanded an inquiry into my conduct?" exclaimed Eustace, joyfully. "It is what I have ever most warmly desired."

"And know you whom you have to thank?" said Sire John. "That youngster who stands at your feet—'twas he that, with little Prince Edward, burst into the council, and let not another word be said till he had told your need, given Fulk Clarenham the lie direct, and challenged him to prove his words. Pray when is the defiance to be fought out, Sir Page?"

Arthur coloured crimson, and looked down; then raising his glowing face, said firmly, "To-morrow, if need were, Sir—for God would defend the right!"

"Roundly spoken, Master Page! But let not your early years be all talk, nothing worth."

"The same warning that you gave to me, Sir John," said Eustace.

"When you thought I looked coldly and churlishly on your new-won honours," said Sir John. "I own I thought the Prince was bestowing knighthood over lightly —and so do I say still, Sir Eustace. But I saw, afterwards, that you were not so easily uplifted as I had thought. I saw you as diligent in the study of all that was knightly as if your spurs were yet to earn, and I knew the Prince had a brave young servant in you."

"If he would have trusted me!" said Eustace.

"He hath been deceived by the flatterers who have gained his ear. It should not have been thus had I been at court; but things have been much against my counsel. It may be that I have been too plain spoken—forgetting that he is not the boy who used to be committed to my charge—it may be that he hath been over hasty—and yet, when I look on his changed mien and wasted face, I can scarce blame him, nor must you, Sir Eustace, though cruel injustice hath, I fear, been done you."

"I blame our glorious Prince!" exclaimed the young Knight. "I would as soon blame the sun in heaven because the clouds hide his face from me for a time!"

"The clouds are likely to be dispersed with a vengeance," said Chandos. "The confession of yonder mutinous traitors will clear you from all that your accusers have said, by proving their villainy and baseness!"

"How? Sanchez and his fellows? Have they surrendered?"

"Yes. They kept themselves shut up in Montfort's tower until they lost all hope of relief from their friends without; then, being in fear of starvation, they were

94

forced to surrender, and came forth, praying that their lives might be spared. I, as you may suppose, would as lief have spared the life of a wolf, and the halters were already round their necks, when your dark-visaged Squire prayed me to attempt to gain a confession from them; and, sure enough, they told a marvellous tale:—that Clarenham had placed them here to deliver you up to the enemy, whom they were to admit by a secret passage—and that they would have done it, long since, save that you and your Squire not only discovered the passage, but showed such vigilance, and so frustrated all their plans, that they firmly believed that you held commerce with the foul fiend. Did you, in truth, suspect their treachery?"

"Yes," replied Eustace, looking at Arthur. "The recognition of Le Borgne Basque in the Seneschal would have been sufficient to set us on our guard."

"But the passage?" asked Sir John, "what knowledge had you of that? for they vow that you could never have discovered it but by art magic."

"We found it by long and diligent search."

"And what led you to search, Sir Eustace? I you can clear up the matter, it will be the better for you; for this accusation of witchcraft will hang to you like a burr —the more, perhaps, as you are somewhat of a scholar!"

"It was I who warned him of it, Sir Knight," said Arthur, stepping forward.

"You, young Page!" exclaimed Sir John. "Are you jesting? Ha! then you must have, page-like, been eaves-dropping!—I should scarce have thought it of you."

"Oh, uncle!" exclaimed Arthur, in great distress, "you do not believe me capable of aught so unknightly? Do but say that you, at least, trust my word, when I say that I learnt their plots by no means unbecoming the son of Sir Reginald Lynwood."

"I believe you fully, Arthur," replied his uncle; "the more, that I should have been the last person to whom you would have brought information gained in such a fashion."

"And how was it gained?" asked Sir John.

"That," said the boy, "is a secret I am bound never to disclose."

"Strange, passing strange," repeated the old Knight, shaking his head. "Clarenham and Ashton would scarce have taken any into their councils who would warn you. And you will or can tell no more?"

"No more," replied the boy. "I was bidden secretly to warn my uncle of the entrance to the vaults, and of the treachery of this villain garrison. I did so, and he who says aught dishonourable of him or of me lies in his throat."

"Can you read this riddle, Sir Eustace?" asked Chandos, looking rather suspiciously at the very faint glow which mantled in the white cheek of the wounded Knight.

"I know nothing but what he has told you, Sir John," replied he.

"Nor guess aught?" said Sir John; "but perhaps that is scarce a fair query; and I will to the rest of my business, though it is scarce needed—only I would have the Prince see the full extent of the falsehoods with which he has been gulled." And he then proceeded to inquire into the circumstances of Lady Eleanor's funeral, the brawling, the violent abstraction of Arthur, and of a considerable portion of his property, and the long delay, which had given his enemies so much opportunity to blacken his character. Eustace explained all fully to the satisfaction of Chandos, and appealed to numerous witnesses.

"That is well," said the old Knight. "We shall have it all clear as daylight;—and the only wonder is, that the Prince could be so long deceived by such monstrous falsehoods. Let me see—your right to the wardship is established?"

"Yes; it hath been so decided by the Bishop of Winchester."

"And let me tell you, Sir Eustace, you did yourself little good by getting the interest of the Duke of Lancaster. Methought it still further prejudiced the Prince."

"It was justice that I sought, not favour," said Eustace.

"The knightly view," said Sir John; "and it was more the work of your friends than yourself; but I never loved that young John of Lancaster, and still less since he hath seemed willing to make a party for himself. I trow he hath given the Prince a distrust of all uncles. Ha! little varlet!" added he, as he met Arthur's eyes —"if you can keep one secret, keep another, or, still better, forget what I have said. Understandest thou?"

"I will answer for him," said Eustace.

"And now," said Chandos, "I must be on my way back; for that expedition to Bescancon must be looked to. But what is to be done with the boy?"

"Oh, I remain here," cried Arthur, eagerly. "The Prince consented. Oh, I pray of you let me stay here."

"In this dismal old Castle, Arthur," said Eustace, "apart from all your playmates? It will not be like home, remember; for scarce ever will you be able to go beyond the walls—and with me lying here, and Gaston always occupied, you will find it weary work."

"Not with you, Uncle Eustace! I shall sit by you, and tend you, and read to you. It is so long since I have been with you! Oh, send me not away! I care for no playmate—for nothing in the wide world, as for you!"

"Well, let him e'en stay," said Sir John; "it will be a better training for him than among the gilded little varlets who are cockered up among Princess Joan's ladies."

The two Knights had next to arrange some matters respecting the garrison; Sir John leaving a sufficient number of men to secure the castle in case of a second attack. He was somewhat inclined to leave Master Henry Neville to command them; but consideration for Eustace and Gaston induced him to spare the young gentleman a sojourn which he would have regarded as so far from enviable. Nor was the leech more desirous of a lengthened stay with a patient whom he suspected to be unable to requite him for the discomfort which he might endure in his service. He therefore pronounced Sir Eustace to stand in no further need of his attentions; and recommending rest, and providing him with good store of remedies, he saddled his mule to accompany Sir John Chandos.

The old Commander took his leave, with many kind wishes for Sir Eustace's speedy recovery, and promises that he should ere long hear from Bordeaux. In ten minutes more Arthur, standing at the window, announced that the troop was riding off, with Clisson's pennon borne among them in triumph, and Sanchez and his accomplices, with their hands tied, and their feet fastened together beneath the bodies of their horses.

CHAPTER XVI

Four or five weeks had passed away since Sir John Chandos had quitted the Chateau Norbelle.

The Knight had nearly recovered his full strength, but still wore his broken arm in a scarf, when, one evening, as he was sitting on the battlements, delighting the ears of Arthur and of Gaston with an interminable romance of chivalry, three or four horseman, bearing the colours and badges of the Black Prince, were descried riding towards the Castle. Knight, Squire, and Page instantly descended to the courtyard, which, in short space, was entered by the messengers, the principal of whom, an elderly man-at-arms, respectfully saluted the Knight, and delivered to him a parchment scroll, tied with silk of scarlet and blue, supporting the heavy seal of the Prince of Wales and Duke of Aquitaine, and addressed to the hands of the honourable Knight Banneret Sir Eustace Lynwood, Castellane of the Chateau Norbelle. This document bore the signature of Edward himself, and contained his mandate to Eustace, to come immediately to his court at Bordeaux, leaving the command of the Chateau Norbelle to the bearer.

The old man-at-arms was closely questioned all the evening respecting the state of the court, but he could give little information. Sir John Chandos was at Bordeaux, and had daily attended the council, to which the Prince was devoting more attention than usual; a vessel had also arrived bearing letters from England to the Prince; this was all the information that could be obtained.

The next morning Eustace, with Gaston, Arthur, and Ingram, all full of expectation, and delighted at the change from the gloomy solitary old Castle, were all posting on their way back to Bordeaux. They slept at an hostel about twelve miles from the town, first, however, by desire of the Prince's messengers, sending Ingram on to announce their speedy arrival, and about ten in the morning rode into town.

There was evidently some grand spectacle at hand, for the Bordelais, gentle and simple, in holiday habits, were proceeding in the direction of the palace; but the Knight and his attendants had no time to wait for inquiries, and pressed on with the stream to the gates of the courtyard, where they found warders placed, to keep back the dense throng of people. At the mention of Sir Eustace's name they readily and respectfully admitted him and his companions into the court.

"Ha!" cried Gaston, "what means this? is there a tilt towards? This reminds me of the good old days, ere the Prince fell ill. The lists, the galleries, the ladies, the Prince's own chair of state, too! Oh, Sir Eustace, I could tear my hair that you cannot yet use your sword arm!"

"Can it be a challenge on the part of Fulk?" said Eustace, "or a reply to yours, Arthur? Yet that can hardly be. And see, there is no barrier in the midst, only a huge block. What can be intended?"

"I do not see Agnes among the ladies in the galleries," said Arthur, looking up as eagerly, and more openly, than his uncle was doing. "And oh, here comes the

Princess,—yes, and Lord Edward and little Lord Richard with her! And here is the Prince himself leaning on the Earl of Cambridge! Uncle Eustace, Lord Edward is beckoning to me! May I run to him?"

"Come with me, since I must present myself," said Eustace, dismounting, as one of the Prince's Squires held his horse.

"And, oh! who is yonder dark-browed dwarfish Knight at the Prince's right hand?" cried Arthur.

Eustace could scarcely believe his eyes, as he looked where the boy pointed.

The royal party were now seated in full array on their raised platform; the Prince upon his chair of state, with more brightness in his eye and of vigour in his movements than when Eustace had last seen him; and at his side sat his wife,—her features still retaining the majestic beauty of Joan Plantagenet, the Fair Maid of Kent—but worn and faded with anxiety. She watched her princely Lord with an eye full of care, and could scarcely spare attention for the lovely child who clung to her side, and whose brilliantly fair complexion, wavy flaxen hair, high brow, and perfectly formed though infantine features, already promised that remarkable beauty which distinguished the countenance of Richard II. On the other side of the Prince sat his sister-in-law, the Countess of Cambridge, a Spanish Infanta; and her husband, Edmund, afterwards Duke of York, was beside the Princess of Wales. But more wonderful than all, among them stood the Constable of France. The two boys, Prince Edward and his cousin Henry of Lancaster, were stationed as pages on each side of the Princess, but as their play-fellow, Arthur, advanced with his uncle, they both sprang down the steps of the gallery to meet him, and each took a hand. Edward, however, first bethinking himself of the respect which, Prince as he was, he owed to a belted Knight, made his reverence to Sir Eustace, who, at a sign from the Prince of Wales, mounted the steps and bent his knee to the ground before him.

"Nay, Sir Eustace," said the Prince, bending forward, "it is rather I who should kneel to you for pardon; I have used you ill, Eustace, and, I fear me, transgressed the pledge which I gave to your brother on the plain of Navaretta."

"Oh, say not so, my gracious liege," said Eustace, as tears gathered in his eyes, —"it was but that your noble ear was deceived by the slanders of my foes!"

"True, Sir Eustace—yet, once, Edward of England would not have heard a slanderous tale against one of his well-proved Knights without sifting it well. But I am not as once I was—sickness hath unnerved me, and, I fear me, hath often led me to permit what may have dimmed my fame. Who would have dared to tell me that I should suffer my castles to be made into traps for my faithful Knights? And now, Sir Eustace, that I am about to repair my injustice towards you, let me feel, as a man whose account for this world must ere long be closed, that I have your forgiveness."

The Prince took the hand of the young Knight, who struggled hard with his emotion. "And here is another friend," he added—"a firmer friend, though foe, than you have found some others."

"Well met, my chivalrous godson," said the Constable du Guesclin, holding out his hand. "I rejoice that my neighbour, Oliver, did not put an end to your *faits d'armes.*"

"I marvel—," Eustace hardly found words between wonder and condolence. The Prince caught the import of his hesitating sentences.

"He thinks you a prisoner, Sir Bertrand," he said. "No, Sir Eustace, Messire le Connetable is captive only in his good-will to you. I wrote, to pray him to send me his witness to those last words of your brother, since you had ever appealed to him, and he replied by an offer, which does us too much honour, to become our guest."

"I am no scribe, apart from my fairy Dame Tiphaine," said Du Guesclin, abruptly. "It cost me less pains to ride hither,—besides that I longed to renew my old English acquaintance, and see justice done to you, fair godson."

"Ha! Sir Bertrand, thou recreant!—so no other spell drew thee hither? Thou hast no gallantry even for such an occasion as this!" said a gay voice.

"How should the ill-favoured Knight deal in gallantries?" said Du Guesclin, turning. "Here is one far fitter for your Grace's eyes."

"And you, discourteous Constable, were keeping him for you own behoof, when all my maidens have been speaking for weeks of no name but the Knight of the beleaguered Castle!"

And Eustace had to kiss the fair hand of the Princess of Wales.

In the meantime, the three boys were whispering together. "It is all well, all gloriously well, is it not, Arthur, as I told you?" said Edward. "I knew my father would settle all in his own noble fashion."

"What said the master of the Damoiseaux?" asked Arthur, as the sight of that severe functionary revived certain half-forgotten terrors.

"Oh, he, the old crab-stock!" said Henry,—"he looked sour enough at first; but Edward kept your counsel well, till you were safe at a good distance from Bordeaux; and then, though he said somewhat of complaining to my Lord the Prince, it was too late to mend it. And when Sir John Chandos came back, and bade him be content, he vowed you were enough to spoil a whole host of pages; but did not we all wish some of our uncles would get themselves betrayed?"

"But what means all this preparation?" asked Arthur—"these lists! Oh, surely, there is not to be a tourney, which I have so longed to see!"

"No," said Edward, "that cannot be, my mother says, while my father is so weakly and ill. But there are the trumpets! you will soon see what will befall."

And, with a loud blast of trumpets, the gorgeously arrayed heralds rode into the court, followed by a guard of halberdiers, in the midst of whom rode a Knight in bright armour, his visor closed, but his shield and crest marking the Baron of Clarenham.

When the trumpets had ceased, and the procession reached the centre of the lists, they halted, and drew up in order,—the principal herald, Aquitaine, immediately in front of the Prince. After another short clear trumpet-blast, Aquitaine unrolled a parchment, and, in a loud voice, proclaimed the confession of Fulk, Baron of Clarenham, of his foul and unknightly conduct, in attempting to betray the person of the good Knight and true, Eustace Lynwood, Knight Banneret, with that of his Esquire, Gaston d'Aubricour, and of certain other trusty and well-beloved subjects of his liege Lord, King Edward of England, together with the fortalice, called Chateau Norbelle, in the county of Gascogne, appertaining to my Lord Edward, Prince of Wales and Duke of Aquitaine, into the hands of the enemy—having for that purpose tampered with and seduced Thibault Sanchez, Seneschal of the Castle, Tristan de la Fleche, and certain others, who, having confessed their crime, have received their deserts, by being hung on a gallows—upon which same gallows it was decreed by the authority of the Prince, Duke and Governor of Aquitaine, that the shield of Fulk de Clarenham should be hung—he himself being degraded from the honours and privileges of knighthood, of which he had proved himself unworthy—and his lands forfeited to the King, to be disposed of at his pleasure.

Clarenham was then compelled to dismount from his horse, and to, first one foot, and then the other, upon the block, where a broad red-faced cook, raising his cleaver, cut off the golden spurs. Sir John Chandos, as Constable of Aquitaine, then came forward, and, taking the shield from the arm of Clarenham, gave it, reversed, into the hands of one of the heralds, who carried it away. The belt, another token of knighthood, was next unbuckled, and Chandos, taking the sword, broke it in three pieces across his knee, saying, "Lie there, dishonoured steel!" and throwing it down by the spurs. Lastly, the helmet, with the baronial bars across the visor, was removed, and thrown to the ground, leaving visible the dark countenance, where the paleness of shame and the flush of rage alternated.

"And now, away with the traitor, away with the recreant Knight! out upon him!" cried in a loud voice Sir John Chandos, while the shout was taken up by a deafening multitude of voices—in the midst of which the degraded Knight and landless Baron made his way to the gate, and, as he passed out, a redoubled storm of shouts and yells arose from without.

"Out upon the traitor!" cried Harry of Lancaster with the loudest. "Away with him! But, Edward, and you too, Arthur, why shout you not? Hate you not traitors and treason?"

"I would not join my voice with the rabble," said Edward, "and it makes me sad to see knighthood fallen. What say you, Arthur?"

"Alas! he is my mother's kinsman," said Arthur, "and I loved his name for her sake as for that of Agnes too. Where is Agnes?"

"In the Convent of the Benedictine nuns," said Edward. "But in your ear, Arthur, what say you to our plan that she shall be heiress of her brother's lands, on condition of her wedding—guess whom?"

"Not mine uncle! Oh, Lord Edward, is it really so? How rejoiced old Ralph would be!"

"Speak not of it, Arthur—it was my mother who told me, when Agnes craved permission to go to the Convent, and I feared she would become one of those black-veiled nuns, and I should never see her more."

"Where is my uncle?" asked Arthur, gazing round. "I thought he was standing by the Lady Princess's chair—"

"He went to speak to Sir John Chandos but now," said Prince Henry, "but I see him not. Mark! what a lull in the sounds without!"

In fact, the various cries of execration which had assailed Fulk Clarenham on his exit from the gates of the Castle, after sounding more and more violent for some minutes, had suddenly died away almost into stillness—and the cause was one little guessed at within the court. The unhappy Fulk was moving onwards, almost as in a dream, without aim or object, other than to seek a refuge from the thousand eyes that marked his disgrace, and the tongues that upbraided him with it; but, in leaving the court, he entered upon a scene where danger, as well as disgrace, was to be apprehended. The rabble of the town, ever pleased at the fall of one whose station was higher than their own, mindful of unpaid debts, and harsh and scornful demeanour, and, as natives, rejoiced at the misfortune of a foreigner, all joined in one cry of—"Away with the recreant Englishman!—down with him!—down with him!" Every hand was armed with a stone, and brief would have been Fulk's space for repentance, had not the cry in its savage tones struck upon the ear of Eustace as he stood in the lists, receiving the congratulations of Sir John Chandos and of other Knights, who, with changed demeanour, came to greet the favoured hero.

"They will murder him," exclaimed Eustace; and breaking from his new friends, he made his way to the gate, and hurried into the town, just as Fulk had fallen to the ground, struck by a heavy stone hurled by the hand of no other than John Ingram. He rushed forward amid the hail of stones, and, as he lifted Clarenham's head, called out, "How is this! Brave men of Bordeaux, would you become murderers! Is this like honourable men, to triumph over the fallen!"

They held back in amazement for a second; then, as Eustace knelt by him and tried to recall his consciousness, murmurs arose, "Why interferes he with our affairs? He is English," and they all held together. "Another of the purse-proud English, who pay no debts, and ruin the poor Bordelais." "His blood we will have, if we cannot have his money. Away, Master Knight, be not so busy about the traitor, if you would not partake his fate."

Eustace looked up as the stones were uplifted, and more than one Free Companion had drawn his sword. "Hold," he exclaimed in a clear full-toned voice that filled every ear. "Hold! I am Eustace Lynwood, the Castellane of Chateau Norbelle!"

There was an instant silence. Every one pressed forward to see him, whose recent adventures had made him an object of much interest and curiosity, and the attention of the crowd was entirely diverted from the former unhappy subject of their pursuit. Whispers passed of "Noble Knight! flower of chivalry! how generous and Christian-like he bends over his enemy! Nay, if he revenge not himself, what right have we? And see, his arm is still in a scarf from the treachery of those villains! Well, I would yet give yon ruffian his desert."

By this time Eustace having observed Ingram among the crowd, summoned him to his side, and at the same time courteously craving the aid of one of the bystanders (who, of course, though collectively lions, were individually lambs), succeeded in conveying Clarenham, whose senses had so far returned that he was able to rise with their assistance, to the door of a monastery chapel, the porch of which opened upon the street.

101

"Holy Fathers," said Eustace, "I crave the protection of the Church for an unhappy, and, I trust, a penitent man, praying you will tend him well to aid and relief alike of body and soul, until you hear from me again."

With these words he quitted the chapel before his late enemy had sufficiently recovered his faculties to recognize his preserver.

Leonard Ashton, for whom Eustace inquired, had, it appeared, saved himself by making full confession, and had been sent home, in deep disgrace, though spared public dishonour.

It was some few days after these events that the presence of Lady Agnes de Clarenham was requested in the parlour of her nunnery, which was some miles distant from Bordeaux, by a person who, as the porteress informed her, was the bearer of a message from the Princess of Wales. She descended accordingly, but her surprise was great on beholding, instead of one of the female attendants of her mistress as she had expected, the slender figure of the young Knight with whom she had last parted at the hostelry.

Her first feeling was not one of kindness towards him. Agnes had indeed grieved and felt indignant when she saw him oppressed and in danger from her brother's treachery, but, in these days of favour, she could not regard with complacency the cause of her brother's ruin, and of the disgrace of her house. She started, and would have retreated, but that he prevented, by saying, in a tone which had in it more of sorrow than of any other feeling, "Lady Agnes, I pray you to hear me—for you have much to forgive."

"Forgive! Nay, Sir Eustace, it is you who have so much to forgive my unhappy house! Oh, can you," she added, as the countenance and manner recalling long past days made her forget her displeasure, "can you tell me where the wretched one has shrouded his head from the shame which even I cannot but confess he has merited?"

"I heard of the Bar—of your brother this very morn," said Eustace, "from one of the good brethren of the Convent where he has taken shelter, the Convent of the Augustine friars of St. Mary; they spoke of him as amended in health, and, though sorely dejected, returning, they hoped, to a better spirit.'

"Thanks, Sir Eustace, even so do I hope and pray it may be—since repentance is the only good which can yet be his. But tell me, Sir Eustace—for vague rumours only reach us in this lonely cell—was it true that the populace pursued the fallen one with clamours, and might even have slain him, but for his rescue by a gallant Knight, who braved their utmost fury?"

"It was even so, Lady," said Eustace, with some embarrassment.

"Oh! who was that noblest of Knights, that I may name him in my most fervent prayers? who has that strongest claim on the gratitude of the broken-hearted sister?"

"Nay, Lady, it was but common duty, the mere mercy of a Christian man, who could not see a fellow-creature die such a death, without attempting to save him."

"Oh, Sir Eustace! it is not like your former self to deny the greatness of a noble deed! I will not be robbed of my gratitude! Tell me the name of that most noble of men!"

He half smiled, then looking down, and colouring deeply: "Do you remember, Lady Agnes, the Knight whom you bound by a promise, that in case of the triumph of his cause—"

"Eustace, Eustace! Oh, I should have known that nothing was too great and high for you, that you would not disparage the nobleness of any other than yourself. Oh, how shall I ever render you my thanks! After such cruel treachery as that from which you have, and, I fear me, are still suffering! Alas! alas! that I should be forced to use such harsh words of my own brother!"

"I trust you may still be comforted, Lady," said Eustace. "From what the good Fathers tell me, there is hope that Fulk may yet be an altered man, and when the pilgrimage to the Holy Land, which he has vowed, is concluded, may return in a holy temper."

"Return; but whither should he return?" said Agnes, in a broken, despondent tone,—"landless, homeless, desolate, outcast, what shelter is open to him? For if the porteress's tale spoke truth, his lands and manors are forfeited to the King."

"They are so, in truth; but there is one way, Agnes, in which they may still be restored to their true owner."

"How so? What mean you, Sir Eustace?"

"Agnes, I would not have broken upon your sorrow by speaking thus abruptly, but that the Prince's, or rather the King's desire was urgent, that the matter should be determined without loss of time. To you, in all justice, does he will that the castles and manors of Clarenham should descend, but on one condition."

Agnes raised her eyes, and, while she slowly shook her head, looked anxiously at him as he paused in considerable embarrassment.

"On condition that you, Lady Agnes, should permit the King and Prince to dispose of your fair hand in marriage."

Agnes gave a slight cry, and leant against the grate of the parlour. "Oh, that may never be, and—but how advantageth that poor Fulk?"

"Because, Lady Agnes—because it is to me that they would grant that hand which I have so long loved passionately and hopelessly. Agnes, it was not willingly, but at the command of the Prince, that I came hither with a suit which must seem to you most strangely timed, from one who has been the most unwilling cause of so much misery to you, whom, from earliest years, he has ever loved more than his own life. I know, too, that you cannot endure to rise on the ruin of your brother, nor could I bear to feel that I was living on the lands of a kinsman and neighbour whose overthrow I had wrought. But see you not, that jointly we can do what we never could do separately, that, the condition fulfilled, we could kneel before King Edward, and entreat for the pardon and restoration of Fulk, which, to such prayers, he would surely grant?"

Agnes' tears were gathering fast, and she spoke in a broken voice, as she said, "Eustace, you are the most generous of Knights," and then, ashamed of having said so much, covered her face with her veil and turned away. Eustace stood watching her, with his soul in his eyes; but before either had summoned courage to break the silence, the porteress came hurrying in, "Good lack! good lack! if ever my eyes saw the like—here is the Princess of Wales herself at the gate, and all her train—where is sister Katherine? where is the mother abbess? Alas, alas! that nought should be ready to receive her! Oh, and I have mislaid the key of the great gate!" While the good woman was bustling on in her career, Eustace had time to say, "Yea, Agnes, the Princess is come, in case you hear my suit favourably, to conduct you back to Bordeaux. Think of a true and devoted heart, think of Fulk ere you decide!" As he spoke, the whole train of black-veiled nuns came sweeping into the parlour, whence Agnes hastily escaped to collect her thoughts during the few instants before she could be summoned to attend the Princess, while Eustace walked into the Convent court, which was by this time filled by the gay party which accompanied the Princess.

Agnes quickly gained her cell, and sank down on her bed to make the most of the minutes that might be her own. Never, probably, had lady shorter time in which to decide, or did it seem more impossible to come to a resolution; but Agnes had known Eustace all her life, had never met one whom she thought his equal, found him raised a thousand-fold in her estimation by the events of the day, and could not bear to think of disappointing the hopes which had lighted up that bright eye and animated that whole face.

Then, too, why by her act completely ruin her brother? The thoughts flashed through her mind in rapid succession, and she did not rise with much reluctance when called to meet the Princess, though longing for more time, which after all would but have enabled her to harass herself more.

"Well, my gentle Agnes," said the Princess, "what say you? Come you back to the court, where my boys are wearing for their playfellow? Hasten, then sweet maiden, for I promised little Edward to bring you back, and I know not how to face his wrath if you come not."

Agnes, still almost dreaming, offered no opposition, but allowed her dress to be arranged, took leave of the abbess and her nuns, and shortly found herself, she scarcely knew how, mounted on her palfrey in the Princess's train, with Sir Eustace Lynwood at her side.

And old Ralph Penrose was one of the happiest of mankind, when he beheld his pupil return the first Knight in the county—the honoured of the Prince.

For the next seven years the Clarenham vassals rejoiced in the gentle, noble, and firm rule of their new Lord and Lady; yet it was remarked, with some surprise, that the title of Baron of Clarenham was dropped, and that Sir Eustace and Dame Agnes Lynwood, instead of living at their principal Castle, took up their abode at a small manor which had descended to the lady from her mother, while the Castle was placed under the charge of Gaston d'Aubricour, beneath whose care the fortifications assumed a more modern character, and the garrison learnt the newest fashions of handling their weapons.

At the end of that time Sir Eustace and his Lady travelled to the court, where, alas! of all the royal party who had rejoiced at their marriage, they found only the Young King Richard II. and his mother, the Princess Joanna, once the Fair Maid of Kent, but now sadly aged by time and sorrow, who received kindly, though tearfully, those who reminded her of those last bright days of her life at Bordeaux, and readily promised to forward their request at the council, "where, alas!" she said, shaking her head, "Lord Henry of Lancaster, now Earl of Bolingbroke, too often loved to oppose her and her son."

No one at the council could refuse, thought the amazement of all was great, when the request was made known that King Richard would be pleased to reinstate in his titles, lands, and manors, Fulk, late Baron of Clarenham, in consideration of his good services to Christendom, rendered on the coast of Africa under the banner of the Knights of St. John, whose Grand Master attested his courage and faithfulness.

Soon Clarenham Castle opened its gates to receive its humbled, repentant, and much-changed Lord, who was welcomed by all the gentle blood in the county—at the head of whom rode Sir Eustace with his Squire, and his nephew Arthur, now a gallant young man, only waiting the summons, promised him by the Princess, to receive knighthood at the same time as his royal master, Richard II.

Made in the USA
Middletown, DE
25 June 2016